GEORGE CHANCE
THE GREEN GHOST

AIRSHIP 27 PRODUCTIONS

George Chance-The Green Ghost Volume 1

"The Phantom Elephant of Coney Island" © 2014 Michael Panush
"The Case of the Ectoplastic Escapist" © 2014 Greg Hatcher
"The Case of the Rocketeer Ripper" © 2014 B.C. Bell
"Murder in Sound Effects" © 2014 Erwin K. Roberts

Published by Airship 27 Productions
www.airship27.com
www.airship27hangar.com

Cover and interior illustrations © 2014 Zachary Brunner

Editor: Ron Fortier
Associate Editor: Gordon Dymowski
Production and design by Rob Davis.
Marketing and promotions manager: Michael Vance

ISBN-13: 978-0615993300
ISBN-10: 0615993303

Printed in the United States of America

10 9 8 7 6 5 4 3 2 1

GEORGE CHANCE

THE GREEN GHOST

VOLUME ONE
TABLE OF CONTENTS

THE PHANTOM ELEPHANT OF CONEY ISLAND

Michael Panush

The decaying amusements of Pixie Park looked like some gaudy graveyard in the evening. The entrance was a small wharf, leading from Brooklyn to Coney Island and the rickety land of piers, crisscrossing wharves, packed booths, and towering rides of the various establishments that supplied New York with its entertainment. Or at least they had before the advent of the cinema and the crushing weight of the Great Depression hit the city. Pixie Park, like many of the old Coney Island dives, had gone under. Now it was abandoned, a strange tombstone for a gaudy couple of decades long vanished. The pier led through an archway that resembling an oversized, smiling mouth. The teeth were falling from the mouth and the paint on the glaring eyes had faded. It seemed like the mouth belonged to someone yawning or maybe emitting a final scream.

George Chance leaned his head against the window of his bottle green Rolls Royce, his eyes darting over the crumbling, faded signs for Pixie Park's greatest attractions. He was in the back, with his chauffeur, friend, and bodyguard Joe Harper behind the wheel. Chance watched the signs go by, the words almost unreadable in the evening's gloom. There was the midway, the rides, which included a skeletal roller coaster and an oversized Ferris wheel, and the freak show. Chance knew about places like Pixie Park, even if they were a bit before of his time. He was a magician and had worked the circuit on his way up, dazzling onlookers with card tricks in Podunk county fairs before hitting the big city. He went big then and wouldn't be caught dead without a packed concert hall in Broadway. But if things had gone differently, if Chance hadn't met the right sort of people and caught the right breaks, he might have ended up in some dead-end, rundown joint like Pixie Park had been right before it closed. That was show business for you. It was tough. Of course, now Chance had a new job with its own unique set of challenges. He couldn't say it was any easier.

The Rolls rode into the open midway. A bit of rain dribbled down from the dark sky and splattered on the dashboard. "For Christ's sake." Harper spat out the words. He had handsome, angular features, with dark hair slicked back and shining. His charcoal suit was never without its diamond

5

stickpin. Harper turned around and glared at Chance. "We really gotta be here, boss? In the rain and all?"

"You don't like it, Joe?" Chance reclined in the cushioned leather seat of the Rolls. He had short, neatly combed blonde hair and a dark green suit, vest, and matching bowtie. His fedora, of the same green shade, rested on his lap. "I thought you were made of sterner stuff."

"I ain't scared," Harper replied. "You know it'll take more than some raindrops and a scary locale to frighten me. It's just that this job is a hassle. Going out in the middle of night, to some dump of a theme park and for what? Cause a bunch of Lucky Leo Lorden's goons reported seeing some ghostly elephant around here. It ain't our business."

Chance shifted in his seat. They were rolling into the midway now, past the various abandoned stalls and games of chance. Back when Pixie Park was still open, these games must have been packed with ring tosses and shooting galleries and Son-of-Ham shows where patrons could pay a nickel and peg a Negro with a baseball for a cheap prize. It must been a riot of noise and color and now it was empty and dead, battered by the rain under the shadow of the roller coaster in the distance. Chance reached into his coat and withdrew his silver cigarette case.

"Indulge me, Joe," Chance replied. "If there's a ghost here, especially the ghost of a monstrous pachyderm, I'd like to see it." He grinned a little as his lighter flashed to life. "Consider it professional curiosity." He pointed up ahead, to the form of an old food stand. "Stop there, Joe, if you would. I think it's time we went out on foot and had a look around."

Harper slowed the Rolls' engine. It went from a growl to a purr. "Sure thing, boss. But you know what they say about curiosity and cats."

"Then we'll just have to do our best to be careful." Chance turned to the fellow sitting next to him as Harper parked the Rolls Royce on the corner of the wooden walkway. "How you doing, Tim?" he asked. "You've been silent since we got here."

Tiny Tim Terry sat next to Chance. He was sitting up, his eyes glued to the window. He was a midget, with a lined face, white hair and pale eyes. In his dark suit, tie and bowler hat, he looked like some strange doll no child would ever want to own. Tiny Tim held one of his cheap nickel cigars in his hand, unlit and forgotten. He was watching Pixie Park too, entranced by the decaying games of the midway. He only looked up when the Rolls came to a stop.

"Been thinking about this place, kid." Tin Tim's voice was deep and scratchy, made hoarse from a lifetime of barking out to milling crowds as he advertised some act or another. He had been in New York for decades and knew Coney Island well. "Pixie Park. Plenty of memories here."

"Did you work in this place?" Chance asked. He moved to open the door and stepped out into the rain. Harper and Tiny Tim hopped out as well. Their shoes settled on the wet pier, splashing in the water. Chance carefully set his fedora on his head. He could hear the rain, drumming on the brim in a constant, gentle beat.

"No." Tiny Tim's reply was curt. He walked over to the nearest stand and glanced inside. "But I knew folks who did. And word was that, even before the park's money troubles started, it was bad. The owners were a bunch of scumbags. Didn't give a damn about the performers or the dangers, as long as the rubes were packed in and they were turning a buck. There was talk of shakedowns, beatings, and worse; not to mention all the fires or injuries from broken equipment." Tiny Tim finally held out his cigar. Chance reached down to light it. The flame seemed tiny against the rain and darkness. "Yeah. I never worked here and I'm glad of it."

The three men started to walk through the midway, moving around the old stands. Everything was quiet apart from the drumming of the rain, the creak of old wood and metal, and the gentle rolling of the ocean against the pier. Chance looked back at his friends. He was glad they had come along. He was a skeptical man, one who had been behind the curtain and knew that almost every ghost or monster was the result of a trick of the light or sleight of hand. As the Green Ghost, it was his duty to use those same tricks to protect the innocent. But the atmosphere of a place wasn't something that could be ignored. And Pixie Park seemed to be brimming with a dark and noxious atmosphere. Chance wished he was at home suddenly, back in Manhattan. There would be a fire there and some warmth. Instead, he was out in Coney Island, looking for the ghost of an elephant.

They walked away from the hulking form of the Rolls, further into the Midway. Harper drew a flashlight from his overcoat and let its beam gleam through the rain and move over the various wooden stands. It illuminated the painted faces of clowns and animals, all distorted by rain and the ravages of time. He switched the light back to Tiny Tim. "So, you saw it, right?" he asked. "Titan the elephant?" He glanced back at Chance. "That's what Lorden's men say they saw; Titan's ghost."

"It'd have to be," Tiny Tim replied. "And I didn't see much of him; only at the end."

Chance wasn't sure of the particulars. "What happened?" he asked. "Exactly?"

Tiny Tim sighed. "Same old story. Titan was this big bull elephant. Maybe they found him in a zoo. Maybe they captured him from Africa, dragged him over when he was a pup. I don't know. Anyway, they had him in this little cage. Not over here; in the freak show. You know what it's like. Steel bars and a barren floor. Maybe they cleaned it once a month, maybe not." He shrugged. "Anyway, one day, a couple of bright sparks decided it would be funny to mess around with Titan. They were these three punks from the city, toughs from Five Points. Back in those days, the Five Points boys did whatever the hell they felt like." He paused and looked at the burning edge of his cigar. "So they started lighting cigarettes and tossing them in. Burning Titan's feet and belly and laughing to beat the band. I guess you can imagine what happened next."

"Titan killed them?" Harper wondered.

"Murdered the lot of them. Just busted out his cage, grabbed one with his trunk and broke the mug's back, skewered another with his tusk and stomped on a third. Just kicked him down and pounded him into paste. You know what a human body looks like when an elephant steps on it? I've seen it once or twice. Ain't pretty."

"I can imagine," Chance replied. "So, they had the poor beast killed?"

"Not just killed," Tiny Tim explained. "Electrocuted. I guess they figured it had to be something special. Or maybe that's how the folks running Pixie Park were; always looking for an excuse to draw a crowd. They put up advertisements all over New York and got a huge turn-out. Sold tons of tickets. This inventor fellow, he was the one who did the electrocuting. Part of proving how his kind of electricity was powerful or a rival's kind was dangerous. Something like that. I don't know." Tiny Tim paused. He jabbed the cigar back between his teeth and blew out a cloud of smoke. "I was there. Just like all the others. Curious enough to see Titan fry."

They came to a gap in the midway. The stalls parted, allowing a small clearing. There was a little stage. Tiny Tim stopped suddenly. His eyes went wide. He dashed over to the stage, his boots splashing in the water. "Yeah!" he called. "It was right here! This very spot! All those years ago." He came to the center of the stage and stopped. "It was something else, I tell you. All them people, crowded together and looking at this stage. And there was Titan, tied up under the spotlights with this cables going to these panels under his feet. The inventor fellow, all dressed in black and with a big top hat, stood there and pulled a switch." Tiny Tim stopped suddenly. The excitement of the memory seemed to slip away from him, replaced by a cold horror. "Then Titan, he kind of sags and just crumples.

No struggle. No trumpeting or trying to break out of his chains. He just crumples. It was strange, seeing something so big and so full of life just stop and collapse. There was this smell too, like overcooked beef left on the grill. I still smell it sometimes."

Tiny Tim stood at the center of the stage, a tiny figure alone in the rain. Moonlight streamed down, illuminating the old decorations around the stage and the roller coaster in the background. Chance could almost imagine it; the great elephant collapsing before an audience and the rush of fear that went through them as they came face to face with the cold reality of death.

"A most disheartening story," Chance muttered.

"Don't I know it," Tiny Tim agreed. "But you know why they killed Titan? The real reason? It's because he didn't play by the world's rules. He just got tired of the abuse he was taking all the time. Couldn't handle it any more. So he went wild and they caught him and they killed him." Tiny Tim rammed his hands in the pockets his little coat. "It's happened before. It'll happen again."

Harper stood at the end of the stage. "And now Titan's ghost is back and terrorizing Lucky Leo Lorden's hatchet-men."

"So runs the theory, anyhow," Chance replied. " But there is something else at work. Leo Lorden's purchase of Pixie Park is curious itself. Why would an up-and-coming Brooklyn kingpin spend his money on purchasing a defunct amusement park? Perhaps he wants to burn it down for the insurance money, but even that could be more trouble than it's worth. And why is Titan's ghost terrorizing his crew? That is another mystery I'd like to solve." He walked over to the stage and stared out at Pixie Park, his eyes drifting by the various exhibitions and entertainments. "The Green Ghost is required, after all, to take in interest in matters dealing with the occult and organized crime. The case of this phantom elephant concerns both."

Then something looked back at Chance from the falling rain and the shadows. They were two shining lights, hovering above the midway. The lights glowed a pale neon blue. They seemed to be coming closer. Then Chance felt a deep rumble coursing through the pier. He glanced down and saw the water in the puddles, now rippling in widening circles. Something was approaching their position; something large. It was closing in fast.

The others noticed it too. "Ah nuts," Harper muttered. "It's Titan, ain't it?" He reached into his coat and withdrew a pearl-handled automatic. Harper knew how to handle a heater. His work as a bouncer and career as a gambler had taught him how to be a good shot. Chance himself wasn't great with a gun, which was one reason why he had brought Harper along.

Chance hopped down from the stage. "Easy there, Joe," he said. "No need for gunfire just yet. In show business, there are few things as important as a good entrance. Let's not spoil it for our newly arrived friend." He reached into his coat and drew out his flashlight. Bravado only went so far. Chance needed to see the source of those baleful blue lights. He snapped his flashlight to life and shone into the rain. "Hello there!" Chance called. "Come out, if you please!"

The rumbling drew closer. Heavy footfalls sounded, loud and pounding like the drums before a battle. A massive shape, standing twice as tall as a man, emerged from the stands and stood before them. It was half-hidden in the rain, with its great dome of a head and long, lean trunk. Two curling tusks reached out, glowing softly in the moonlight. Heavy feet pounded and carried the elephant forward. The blue eyes glowed and shone down on Chance, Tiny Tim, and Harper. Chance couldn't make out most of the elephant, not with the pounding rain and the shadows of night. Titan stood before them and a fearsome trumpet, a loud and terrible whine, cut through the air. The pounding feet continued. Titan was moving into a charge.

"Boss?" Harper spun around. "What do we do?"

"I would suggest an immediate departure," Chance replied. He hopped off the stage, helped Tiny Tim down and then began to bound back to the midway. Harper kept his pace and the three men ran straight for the midway attractions. With another harsh bellow, Titan gave chase. The elephant careened around the stage and headed straight for them, its heavy footfalls pounding out in the same regular time. Titan was hard on their trail and gaining fast.

They cut into the midway and started running back to the Rolls Royce. Chance weaved around a shooting gallery. Harper slipped on a puddle and Tiny Tim grabbed his waist and steadied him. They kept running. Titan reached the shooting gallery and didn't bother charging around the obstacle. Instead, the elephant plowed straight into the flimsy wooden structure. It was like a knife hacking into a chunk of wood. Splinters and fragments of the building flew through the air. Titan kept coming, crashing through another stand and shattering it. Chance doubled his pace, his boots splashing in the water as he tried to gain more ground. Harper and Tiny Tim raced along with him. Up ahead, the green form of the Rolls Royce was scarcely visible through the falling rain. Chance made for it.

Harper turned around. He was still clutching his automatic. "All right," he said. "Here's a peanut for you!" He turned around and fired, cracking off three quick shots before turning and continuing to run. Chance turned to see the effect of the bullets. The automatic shots should have at least caused an elephant to stop and deal with sudden pain. But Titan ignored the bullets. They crashed into the elephant's front. Each shot rose up a torrent of sparks. Chance stared at the bright pinpricks of light flashing against the darkness.

"Metal!" he announced. "Joe, our ghostly elephant is made of metal!" He smiled a little like the knowledge had given him victory.

"Whatever it's made of, it'll still crush us!" Tiny Tim pointed out. "Keep moving!" He pointed ahead to the safety of the Rolls Royce. "We get in that, maybe we can drive to safety!" Titan pounded even closer and smashed his way through some ancient cotton candy stand. Bits of glass and chunks of wood rained down and pelted the boardwalk. Chance gritted his teeth and kept running. Harper and Tiny Tim were at his sides. They raced away from the midway and then the Rolls Royce was right in front of them. Harper slammed open the door and dove into the front seat.

Chance and Tiny Tim barreled into the back as Harper revved the engine. "What about the tools we brought?" Chance asked. "The special equipment for handling an elephant; perhaps we can produce them and take this pachyderm down?"

"Not a chance!" Harper muttered. "Not when it's charging straight for us like this!" He slammed down on the gas pedal. Chance was pushed back into his seat as the Rolls shot down the boardwalk. Great plumes of water shot out from the wheels and flanked the auto like a translucent set of wings. Chance checked the window. Titan hadn't given up yet.

The elephant bashed his way out of the midway and continued its blind charge. Chance still couldn't make out many details about the pachyderm; not the stony gray skin or the oversized ears. He only saw the dark outline, the protruding tusks and the glowing blue eyes. Titan raced after the Rolls, moving into a gallop as the engine revved. As Chance watched, the glowing blue eyes got closer and closer. There was no doubt about it. The elephant was gaining.

"Can we outrun him?" Tiny Tim demanded. "Come on, kid. Make this machine fly!"

"I'm trying. These goddamn puddles are ruining any chance of driving straight." Harper was clenching the wheel. He twisted it to the side and the Rolls slid across the soaking boardwalk. Harper slammed on the brakes and narrowly avoided smashing into another stall. Then he hit the engine again and they roared out, leaving the midway behind. Harper's eyes darted to the rear view mirror. "Ah no," he muttered. "Ah nuts."

"We won't be making our escape from Titan, will we?" Chance asked. He was staring up ahead.

They hadn't quite reached the Ferris wheel and the roller coaster. Instead, they were nearing a large square structure decorated with a pair of outstretched lions outside the door. 'Arcade' was splayed above the door in garish red letters. The headlights of the Rolls shone over the front of the building, illuminating the crumbling teeth of the lions.

Harper glanced at him. "No, boss," he admitted. "We're not."

Titan bashed into them. The metal of the Rolls squeaked and whined under the impact. A tusk stabbed in through the back window. Chance leaned to the side and barely avoided impalement. The force of the impact hurled the Rolls Royce forward. The tires squeaked across the boardwalk and then left the ground altogether. Harper was shouting something. Tiny Tim was struggling to hold onto his seat. The whole automobile flew through the closed doors of the arcade, spun the side and crashed hard into a pillar.

The force of the crash rocketed through the vehicle. Chance banged into the door and it came open. He braced himself but striking the ground and rolling twice still battered his bones and muscles. Still, he'd done escape acts plenty of times. This could just be some new stunt. Chance slid to a stop and then looked up and stared around. He glanced back at the car. Harper was slouched in his seat, still recovering. Tiny Tim was half out of his door, in similar straits. Neither of them seemed to be seriously injured. Chance stared back, into the shadows and rain beside the door. The baleful blue eyes of Titan's ghost were gone. The elephant, ghost or metal or whatever it was, had left.

With a groan, Chance came to his feet. He was standing in the center of small arcade. Wooden games of chance, a little bowling alley, a strength-tester and more activities were set around in the corners. Most were crumbling and falling apart. At least the roof, though broken in several places, offered a slight relief from the rain. Chance removed his fedora and listened to the gentle drip as rain fell from his shoulders and pelted to the ground. Then he heard another noise, coming from the shadowy corners of the arcade. It was a growl. Chance shivered slightly.

They had avoided the elephant or whatever it was but maybe worse danger was right around the corner.

Titan bashed into them.

Rain pounded down on the roof of the arcade. Chance had dropped his flashlight in the frenzied run from Titan's ghost. The odd machines of the arcade seemed distorted in the shadows, like bits of furniture with impossible pieces. Chance did his best to clear his head. There was no time to be frightened, no time to be wowed by the scenery. They were in a dangerous situation and it could easily get worse. The Green Ghost had to be ready.

He thought quickly over what had happened. Titan, if that's what the elephant was, had them at his mercy. He could have charged in and stomped Chance flat. But instead, the maddened pachyderm phantom had turned away and left. It was odd behavior and more evidence that there was a human hand behind Titan's appearance and that human hand hesitated from shedding blood. Chance filed the information away. They had other concerns at the moment.

"What now?" Chance asked. He took a step back to the car. The headlights were still on, making all the shadows in the arcade shift and dance. Chance moved next to Harper as the growl came again. It was a deep and hungry noise, full of anticipation. Chance patted his chauffeur's shoulder. Harper stirred slightly. He sat up and rubbed his forehead, then stared up at Chance.

"Elephant gone, boss?" he asked.

Chance nodded. "Seems to have pushed us in here and fled. But I hesitate to think we are safe." He glanced back at Tiny Tim. The midget was also sitting up. "Tim? Are you well?"

"I've taken worse hits than this," Tiny Tim replied. "And all in the name of show business."

"Well, at least we've got a more worthy goal tonight." Chance looked back at the shadows. "However, our inquiry will be stalled unless we get another look at the mysterious Titan. I am certain that he's not paranormal in nature, nothing really is, after all, and he is only a mystery that needs solving."

With a sigh, Harper opened the door and stepped out. "Go after the elephant? You gone bughouse, boss? Ghost or no ghost, Titan was nearly scraping us off his feet. I don't know if we're up to chasing him down again."

"We have our tools," Chance explained. "And we'll be prepared." He looked at Harper, who still seemed a little upset at this whole endeavor. "Joe, I know you think this is a waste of time but Lucky Leo's activities are important to the future of New York and we need to know all the ins and outs. Otherwise, we can't protect the innocent."

"Spare me the sermon, boss." Harper shrugged. "Long as we're hunting the big game instead of Titan hunting us, I think we'll be okay."

"Excellent. Now, I suggest we leave this area immediately and resume our..."

A striped form lunged out of the shadows. Chance saw it coming, emerging into the circle of illumination cast by the headlights. He recognized the tawny limbs and curved claws, the round head and curved fangs in a split-second. It was a tiger. There was a tiger, leaping straight for him. Chance had no time to wonder where the tiger had come from or what it was doing here. Instead, he launched himself to the side and leapt into the air. The tiger pounced past him, struck the wooden floor and slid. Chance hit the floor next and came to a sudden stop. He turned back. The tiger was facing him. Another growl was coming from inside the arcade.

Harper went for his pistol. "Out of the frying pan and into the fire, eh, boss?" he asked.

"You ain't worried, kid?" Tiny Tim asked.

"Hell, no. These cats are flesh and blood; not ghost or metal. And they'll go down when I put a bullet in them." Harper took aim, but then another tiger leapt from the shadows and landed hard on the roof of the Rolls Royce. Tiny Tim grabbed Harper's hand and yanked him back, pulling him out of the way as the second tiger dropped down with its hungry mouth open. The tiger started pawing towards them and Chance knew that his friends would be busy. He'd have to take care of his own tiger by himself.

He stared back at the big cat. It faced him, its hungry eyes focused on his motion. Chance studied the tiger and realized something: the jungle predator was old. Its fur seemed to thin, there was a scrawniness to it, and even its whiskers drooped. Still, even an old tiger could tear him open in a matter of seconds. Chance took a step back. He glanced over his shoulder, looking for some means of holding off the tiger until he could reach the trunk of the Rolls and his weapons and equipment. Something caught his eye and then the tiger pounced again.

This time, Chance flipped back. He hurled himself into the air and spun. It was an acrobat's trick, normally done on a padded surface or above a net. Chance hit the ground instead and rolled out of the way as the tiger leapt for him. He heard its claws clicking down, inches from his face. Then Chance sprang up and ran. He dashed across the arcade and ran to the test-your-strength stand. A heavy hammer, a sledge, was resting at the bottom. It was covered in dust and looked ancient but an old hammer could still hit. Chance reached out and grabbed the handle. He spun and faced the tiger as it charged for him.

There was no time to swing the heavy mallet around and drive it into the tiger. Instead, Chance grabbed the handle and jabbed the end straight into the tiger's tawny chest. The rounded wood sunk into the fur and pushed the tiger back. Chance felt his muscles strain. He had raced through the rain, blundered through a midway in the dark, and been hurled out of a moving car. His arms ached and he could feel the weight of the sledgehammer, dragging down his arms and slowing his reaction. He gritted his teeth as he prepared to strike again just as the tiger moved to pounce.

Chance saw the striped form of the tiger leaping through the air, claws outstretched. The heavy iron head of the mallet rushed to hit the tiger but the cat was seconds faster. A claw slashed down and batted the mallet from Chase's hands. Another claw punched into his chest and knocked him back to the ground. Chance looked up into the golden eyes of the tiger; saw the fur glowing softly in the headlights. The jaws opened and began to descend. Behind him, Chance heard shouts and cries from Harper and Tiny Tim. He couldn't make out what they were saying but at the moment, it didn't really matter. The tiger was going to lean down and take a bite out of his face and there wasn't a goddamn thing he could do about it. Chance watched the fangs draw closer.

"Ali! Raja!" A deep and resonant voice echoed through the arcade. The tiger paused. Its mouth was still open. "Come over now! Leave those men alone! Come over here! Right now!" The voice was harsh and spoke loudly. There was perhaps a trace of an accent, foreign and exotic, even if the English words were spoken with no trouble. At the moment, Chance didn't care.

He stared back at the tiger and watched as it slipped back. Its claws retracted as it carefully removed its bulk from Chance's chest and sat down on its haunches. Chance's hand rushed over his chest, wondering if he'd find blood and intestines on his suit. Instead, there was only a little torn cloth. He breathed a sigh of relief and came slowly to his feet. Quickly, Chance turned to the Rolls and his friends. The second tiger was pacing back, its long tail swishing back and forth. Tiny Tim and Harper were unharmed. Harper had his automatic in his hand and was pointing it into the shadows of the arcade, towards the direction of the voice.

The tigers headed for the one who had called them as well. They walked past the arcade machines, their claws clicking slightly on the ground. Then they came to sit in front of the figure like a pair of oversized watchdogs. A weathered hand fell on the head of each tiger, giving them a gentle pet. Chance watched as the man who commanded the tigers stepped into view. He was an elderly Negro, with deep black skin and graying hair. A flat cap topped his head and he wore a faded checkered coat and a shirt with a band collar. He was short too, standing just a little taller than Tiny Tim. There was a kind of strength in his wiry arms that Chance could see as he petted the tigers. The cats clearly respected this old man. Chance had to know why.

He took a step towards the old fellow; hand outstretched, and put on his best showman's smile. "Well, sir," he said. "It seems you saved us from becoming tiger chow. I must thank you. My name is George Chance, of Broadway fame, and this is my driver, Mr. Harper and my associate, Tim Terry." He tried to think of a good, plausible explanation that wouldn't reveal the Green Ghost. "I'm a student of decaying architecture and thought it would be a swell little jaunt to tour Pixie Park. I'm afraid I was mistaken." He grinned. "Nobody warned us about the park's wildlife."

The old Negro scratched his chin. "We don't get many visitors here. Not anymore." He walked over to Chance and shook his head. "Name's Benga. I live here."

"Alone?" Tiny Tim wondered.

Benga nodded quickly. "All alone. Just me and the cats."

Harper stared at the tigers. "Just you and the wild animals? Must be a little odd, buddy."

"Not so odd. For several years, I lived in a cage with monkeys."

Chance looked in amazement at Benga. "You're kidding."

"I wish I was." Benga pointed outside. "The ghost elephant is there, lurking outside. Titan is a cruel beast, as wild as he was in life. You should get in your automobile and drive away. Leave Pixie Park behind and never return." Chance looked at Benga's eyes. He wasn't buying the old man's stories. Benga was hiding something. "Do your sightseeing elsewhere. You will find nothing here."

Tiny Tim stepped closer to Benga and looked him over. "You know," he said. "I think I saw you." He stroked his chin. "You used to work here, you say?"

"I was placed in a cage with monkeys and chimps," Benga replied. His eyes went cold. "I am a pygmy, from the Congo, claimed by Belgium. I had a family once but the Force Publique and their rhinoceros-hide whips put an end to that. Then an American explorer offered me passage to America. I thought it would be a better land. Instead, they put me in a cage. Called me some sort of 'missing link'; treated me as though I was not human." He spat. "I spent years here in Pixie Park, living with the monkeys and being tossed peanuts from passerby. Sometimes they let me out. Sometimes they didn't. But it was a cruel place and no one should visit again."

"Jesus," Harper muttered. "They can do that to a guy?"

Tiny Tim shrugged. "He was different from them so that meant they can do anything they want. I've seen if often enough." He looked back at Benga. "So now you live here, taking care of the tigers? Seems a bit odd. This place must harbor some bad memories. Why don't you up stakes and skedaddle?"

"Where would I go? Back to Africa? There is nothing for me in my former home. Not anymore. In this place, at least, I can find peace." Benga shook his head suddenly, like he was an actor remembering his lines. Once more, he pointed to the Rolls Royce. "You shouldn't have come here. Get in your car, Mr. Chance. Drive away."

But Tiny Tim had an idea and Chance knew that his friend wasn't one to let it go. "Say," Tiny Tim continued. "You know a woman named Delores Douglas? About my size? Went by the stage name of Thumbelina? She used to breathe and eat fire while I while I juggled in our old sideshow act in the traveling carnival and then she went to work here. You ever run across her?"

"Delores..." Benga smiled slightly. It seemed like he wasn't trying to frighten them off anymore. "Yes. I do know here. She was one of the few people in Pixie Park who was kind to me. She would make sure I got good food, slipping it through the bars if needed, and would try and sneak me out and take me into the city. She's a good woman."

"So she's still around?" Tiny Tim asked.

Quickly, Benga shook his head. "No. There's nobody left from the old days. It is only me and these old tigers and the ghost of Titan the mad elephant; who is soon to return. Please get into your car and leave before he comes back and smashes both of you into paste."

Now Chance was sure that Benga had something to hide. He was slapping down misdirection, a major magical talent that Chance knew well. Benga didn't want to tell them a thing about Pixie Park. He just wanted them to get into the Rolls and scram and he was using the threat of Titan's ghost to get them moving. Chance wasn't buying it. Still, he supposed it was best to get the Rolls out of the arcade and back onto the pier. No need to be inside this dark building with the old arcade games and a pair of tigers.

He turned to Harper. "Get the car started and back out. We'll join you outside."

"We leaving?" Harper asked. "Finally gonna dangle from this rotten amusement park?"

"I did not say that," Chance corrected. "But back the auto out, if you please."

Harper shrugged and got behind the wheel. He put it in reverse and slid out through the open door. Chance and Tiny Tim walked after him. As they left, Chance glanced back at Benga. The old Negro was watching them from the door. He was biting his lip and seemed unsure. Benga had tried to scare them off and failed. Chance didn't know why, though it must have something to do with Titan's ghost. He didn't want to strong-arm Benga as the old fellow had suffered enough in his lifetime. Plus, there were the two tigers who seemed to obey his commands. Still, he hadn't exactly threatened them and he liked Tiny Tim's old acquaintance Delores Douglas. Maybe Chance could change his mind. Perhaps it would only take a small dose of the truth.

The Rolls Royce rolled back out into the rain. Chance motioned for Harper to stay there and then headed over to Benga. The old man was standing in the doorway, watching them. Tiny Tim was a bit ahead of him, staying in the arcade's awning to avoid the rain. "Look, Mr. Benga," Chance said. "I'm not exactly some tourist looking for odd thrills. I'm operative of the law, in a fashion, and I'm curious about Lucky Leo Lorden's interest in Pixie Park."

"Don't know nothing about that," Benga said. "Nothing at all."

"And I'll tell you something else, sir," Chance continued. "I don't believe in ghosts. I've been in plenty of séances and watched the medium tapping under the table. I've found hidden projectors and bits of smoke and colored gas that help bilk widows out of their fortunes. In fact, on Broadway, I've pulled off plenty of tricks myself." He paused and watched Benga. The expression on the old man's face hadn't changed. "So I don't think Titan's ghost is rampaging around this place, stomping on everyone who comes in. As a matter of fact, Titan hasn't actually killed anyone at all. He banged up our car, but shied away from finishing us off. And none of Lorden's thugs were harmed either when they came here on their various sorties. That's hardly the work of a mad elephantine specter." He folded his arms. "So, Mr. Benga, would you care to tell me what's really going on in Pixie Park?"

Benga pointed behind Chance. "Don't believe in ghosts?" he asked. "Then have a look."

Chance turned. In the darkness, beyond the Rolls, two glowing blue lights shone down. The boardwalk began to rumble and the growing puddles started to ripple. Something big was coming. Immediately, Chance knew it was Titan. He felt a bit of doubt, cold and alien, in the back of his mind. But then he remembered the sparks and the way Titan had shied away from destroying them completely. The elephant form he saw, stepping into the falling rain and drawing closer, was physical. That meant it would be perfectly vulnerable to the tools he had brought.

A few steps brought Chance to the trunk. He snapped it open as Harper stepped out of the car. "Joe!" Chance cried. "We have come prepared and now it is time to show our strength." Chance reached inside, his hand moving through the equipment that they had brought. Before them, Titan gave an ominous trumpet and started to charge. "Now, where is it?" Chance asked to himself. His fingers moved past his costume and equipment needed to become the Green Ghost.

Harper took a step back. "Boss..." he started, "It's charging!"

Sure enough, Titan was breaking into a mad run. The elephant rushed through the falling rain, its trunk swinging this way and that. Behind Benga, the two tigers started to growl and roar. Titan drew closer. Chance could see the glow from the headlights on the tusks. The two blue eyes shone down like a pair of colored suns. His hands danced through the trunk and then he found it. Chance reached in and withdrew an elephant gun; a high-powered express rifle that he had borrowed from one of New York's premier safari clubs. The elephant gun was a powerful and ornate weapon, inlaid with ivory and packing big enough bullets to put down even the largest animal. It was already loaded. Chance considered shooting at Titan himself, but decided against it. Harper was the better shot.

"Right!" Chance cried. "Here you are, Joe. Take that brute down!" He tossed the rifle into the air.

Harper caught it. He cocked the elephant gun and brought it to his shoulder, then stared down the sights at the charging elephant. Now that Harper had a powerful firearm in his hand, his fear seemed to vanish. "I've got him, boss," Harper said. "Where do you want the shot?"

Titan was closing in now, with no signs of stopping. Chance considered it as the elephant galloped into view. Then he saw more the pachyderm's body; saw the steel and the gears in the legs and knew that putting a round into the head or belly of the beast would be a bad idea. He cupped his hands over his mouth and shouted the order to Harper. "The knee, if you please!" he cried. "Put a single shot through the elephant's knee!"

"Got it." Harper took aim. The elephant gun swiveled to face the knee. Then Harper pulled the trigger and the elephant gun rumbled. It was a fantastically loud shot, which seemed to echo all over Pixie Park like sudden and terrible thunder. Chance saw the result of the shot. The bullet tore into the knee, shattering steel, and making a joint break apart. The elephant kept charging, even as its leg came apart and broke beneath the knee.

Then the entire creature collapsed. As it went down, Chance and the others saw what it really was. There was no ghost falling before the blazing headlights of the Rolls Royce. Instead, it was only a strange sort of machine. It appeared to be a kind of moving sculpture, an odd sort of vehicle with four bulky legs in the shape of an elephant. Rusted metal formed the round chest of the elephant, held in place with fat nails driven into ridges of steel. The tusks were shining brass. The eyes were electric and they flickered as the metal elephant collapsed. The legs of Titan seemed strangely spindly. Chance almost wondered how they could hold the bulky elephant upright. The whole conveyance was spotted with rust and seemed very old. Faded paint graced it sides. Advertisements must have been there, sometime in the elephant's past. They were faded into nothingness and now Titan was finished for good.

Titan's head tilted down. Its tusks stabbed into the wood of the boardwalk. They stuck there and the head remained while the rest of the elephant's body went down. The other legs buckled and flapped back and forth like a marionette controlled by a crazed puppeteer. The round belly rolled to the side. Then the metal seams in the belly split and fell open. It cracked like an egg, splitting into two halves. One half rolled aside and came to a rest, still spinning slightly under the rain. The other half pointed upwards. Chance stood on his tiptoes and peaked inside. There was a little room in there; a cockpit for the vehicle. A lever, gears, buttons and more stood at one side, as well as a small viewing window. Everything was miniaturized, designed for children. But the three figures who scrambled from the broken remains of the elephant weren't children at all. Like Tiny Tim Terry, they were midgets.

For a few seconds, the three midgets stood staring at Chance, Harper, Tiny Tim, and Benga. There were two men and one woman who had emerged from the elephant. All three of them were fairly old. One of the men had a pair of pince-nez spectacles and wore overalls with a kerchief tied around his neck. The other was in vest and shirtsleeves and sported a toothpick, which projected from the corner of his bulldog-like mouth. The woman seemed slightly delicate, but there was a hardness to her as well. Her gray hair was wrapped up in a tight bob and she wore a neat checkered dress. She was the first on her feet and her eyes darted over Chance and his allies.

She was the first to speak. Her voice was weathered but strong enough to be heard over the downpour. "Timothy Terry," she said. "Tiny Tim."

"Delores Douglas!" Tiny Tim cried happily. "As I live and breathe!" He hastened to her, running from the arcade and racing into Delores's arms. They hugged quickly. "My God, Delores, you look lovely. It's been far too long since I've seen you. Far too long."

"And you look wonderful as well, Tiny Tim. That's a fetching suit, I must say." Delores patted his shoulder and stepped back. Her smiled remained on her face for a few more seconds and then her hand lashed out and slapped across Tiny Tim's face. "And now you've doomed us, Timothy! You've doomed us all when you destroyed Titan!"

The blow seemed to sting. Tiny Tim stepped back. "Easy there, Delores. You were gonna run right into us. You think we would have just stood there and gotten trampled?"

"I would have stopped!" Delores exclaimed. "It was just supposed to scare you, to make you afraid and send you running away from Pixie Park. But you didn't scare and you destroyed Titan and now we're all good and screwed." She pointed to Tiny Tim. "You cooked our goose, Timothy. We're finished now."

Chance was still trying to make sense of what was happening. He stepped next to Delores. Even though he had to look down at her, he still tried to be as respectful as he could. "Pardon me, ma'am," he said. "I'm George Chance, traveling magician of some note, and Tiny Tim is my associate." He indicated Harper with a nod. "And that's Joe Harper, my driver. I believe that you already know Mr. Benga over there by the arcade entrance."

Benga waved to Delores. "I'm sorry, Delores," he said. "I tried to scare them off. They wouldn't listen."

Harper had slung the elephant gun over his shoulder. He walked over to stand next to Chance. "So you were trying to bamboozle us?" he asked. "Terrify us with that robot elephant and send us packing? Why exactly would you do that?" Then he pointed to Benga. "And you, you said you were the only one living here and that Delores ain't around. But there they

"Delores Douglas!" Tiny Tim cried happily.

are." He folded his arms. "I think you need to come clean. All of you."

Delores spoke slowly, like she was talking to a child. "We did try to scare you off. We do that to everyone who comes into Pixie Park. Mostly, it's just a couple of punk kids daring each other to deal with an elephant's ghost. But lately, Lucky Leo Lorden has been sending his gunsels to check out the place. We scare them off and that's that." She pointed to the ruined form of Titan. "This was an old, moving advertisement some kook built in the Twenties. We spruced it up a bit, made it a little more comfortable and put it to use." Then her lips pursed. "But you guys wrecked the machine and that's all over now."

"I still am unsure on one particular matter," Chance explained. "Why? Why don't you want anyone coming into Pixie Park?"

That made Delores sigh. "It's a long story, Mr. Chance."

"It's been a long night, Miss Douglas," Chance explained. "And it will still be a while before morning. Perhaps we can go somewhere out of this rain and discuss it." He held out his hand. "I apologize for destroying the elephant. In my business, it often pays to fire bullets at phantoms. But I am a gentleman of considerable means. Perhaps I can set it right."

"I doubt it," Delores replied.

"You don't know, Mr. Chance, Delores," Tiny Tim explained. "He's a regular wizard."

"We'll see." Delores pointed to the wreck of Titan. "Okay. See if you can load some of that onto your automobile. Then follow me to the edge of the park, right over the water. You'll see the secret of Pixie Park, such as it is, and you can draw your own conclusions." She paused and then glared at Tiny Tim. "And Timothy? You still smoke those nickel cigars? I'd like one of those, if you don't mind. I think I deserve it."

Tiny Tim busied himself readying the cigar while Benga, Harper, and Chance got to work salvaging what they could of Titan. Chance set the elephant's head on the roof of the Rolls and rested the legs on the back. Harper could drive slowly and the metal elephant pieces would stay on. Chance thought about Delores as he worked. Like Benga and Titan she had been stuck in Pixie Park, trapped on a stage because she was different. Her life had probably been full of hardship. Now he had only made it worse. Chance shook the notions from his head. He didn't know the full story. Delores was going to tell it to him and he had a bad feeling that he wasn't going to like it.

They followed Delores's instructions and drove to the edge of the park, past the motionless Ferris wheel and roller coaster and over to the edge of the dock. The Rolls Royce trundled slowly past the crumbling railing of the boardwalk. There was the cold Atlantic in the distance, swelled with water in the rain. Beyond that, Chance could make out the various lights of New York, shimmering like distant stars. Harper drove carefully and maneuvered the overburdened Rolls Royce over the wharf. As they drove, the rain began to fade. It went from a merciless torrent to a cold drizzle. In the distance, Chance could see shafts of light cutting through the clouds in the sky. The sun was rising. Then, right by the entrance, Chance saw what had to be their destination. He smiled a little at the great coincidence of it all.

They were heading to an elephant. It was a large two-story hotel that resembled a giant wooden elephant. The heavy legs of the elephant rested on the dock and a little stairwell led up to a round door in the middle of the pachyderm's belly. The trunk of the elephant hung down and nearly touched the boardwalk. There was a palanquin on the back, covered with glass so it resembled a miniature lighthouse. The paint on the elephant was peeling and it appeared to be sagging slightly. It was like the elephant was tired and just wanted to fold its legs up and lie down for a long nap. Chance looked over the elephant hotel. He knew there were similar structures set around the east coast. He'd even seen the one in Atlantic City. But this elephant hotel seemed to be permanently closed to outside business. However, lights did burn inside the windows set in the elephant's upper chest and eyes. The hotel was occupied after all.

Delores walked to the hotel and waved to Harper, who killed the engine on the rolls and brought the car to a stop. Chance stepped outside. He had ridden in the back of the automobile alone, giving Tiny Tim a chance to walk alongside Delores. Tiny Tim seemed to be grateful for the opportunity to catch up with an old friend. Now, Chance stepped outside and back into the rain. Benga walked over and stood next to him as Harper left the car as well. The two tigers, who had padded after Benga, suddenly darted for the feet of the elephant hotel. They sprang out like a pair of tawny lightning bolts, making no noise as they scampered across the wet boardwalk.

Another shape emerged from under the elephant. It trundled forward and then stood tall on two hind legs. Chance saw the dark fur and black muzzle and realized that it was a powerfully built black bear, wearing a small red vest. The bear sank down to its haunches and the tigers bounced around it. The tigers opened their mouths and began to make playful growls and whines. The bear joined in. Chance thought they might be fighting for a little, but then saw how gentle the bear's paws were as it tussled with the tigers. They were playing, like a pair of dogs with too much excitement. It was a strange scene and Chance turned back to Benga with a grin.

Benga was smiling too. "No matter how old animals get," he explained. "They still like to play."

Then the door to the elephant hotel creaked open. A strange assortment of people and animals stepped out into the rain to welcome Delores and the others. First, there was a small stream of monkeys. They rushed down and circled the playing bear and tigers, then began to climb up the legs of the elephant hotel. Some of the monkeys wore little vests or sported hats; all of which were faded and old. After them, a pair of Siamese twin sisters emerged, wearing matching kimonos. They had wrinkled faces and gray hair cut short and fused with copious amounts of pomade. Each twin extended a large umbrella to shield the pair from the rain. Next came a tattooed man, naked to the waist despite the cold and covered in intricate, interlinked illustrations. His painted flesh was wrinkled and sagged, making his pictures nearly illegible. He was followed by a bearded lady, her hair snow white and carefully braided into ringlets. A fellow with no lower body emerged. He uses his hands, each finger draped in shining rings, to walk down the steps. Chance stood back and watched them all.

There were a few more midgets and dwarves and a single, swaybacked giant. All of them were old and tired, their days on the stage far behind them. They came down to stand in a little phalanx before Delores and the others. Delores moved to them and talked quietly. She clasped hands and talked in quiet little whispers like she was the mayor of this strange settlement. Chance stood back and looked at the people and animals and then the hotel. He quickly figured out what was going on in Pixie Park and why Titan's ghost seemed so intent on keeping away intruders.

He turned to Benga. "You really were lying about living here alone, Mr. Benga," he said. "There's a whole community, a whole town, of these aging performers from Pixie Park's golden age." He pointed to the hotel. "And you've just been living here, staying in this hotel, as the years pass by?" He shook his head at the thought. "My god, man. How do you manage it?"

"It's not so bad," Benga explained. "We have each other and our friendships. We have little, but what we have, we share. There are some funds, hidden away from the old days. Every so often, one of us goes into town and buys supplies." He smiled a little as he continued. "And what use do we have for the outside world? What has it ever done for us, besides put us in cages and laugh? So we stay here and grow old and the rest of the world can go to Hell, for all we care."

Harper's eyes darted over the residents of the elephant hotel. "A geriatric freak show," he muttered. "How about it, boss? Must be pretty weird around Thanksgiving when all the oddities come and…" He stopped when he saw Tiny Tim glaring at him. Harper grinned weakly and wisely fell silent.

"They've turned their backs on the world," Tiny Tim explained. He looked at Chance. "You know what, kid? I sympathize. Plenty of times I wish I could do the same."

Delores finished talking to her friends. She walked over to join Chance, Harper, and Tiny Tim. "I told them everything would be all right," she explained. "I told them it was nothing but a momentary setback. But I think I might have told a lie." She pointed to Titan's head, still resting on top of the Rolls Royce. "We need that elephant. Titan's ghost has protected this place. It's kept us safe for years and with one bullet you've taken that away from us." Delores's voice dropped to a hateful whisper. "Titan's gone now. There's nothing to stop Lucky Leo's mob from coming in here and throwing us out."

"But why do you have to be here?" Harper asked. "Ain't the most comfortable place, after all."

"Where else would we go?" Delores asked. "What work is there for a bunch of aging freaks; especially with the economy the way it is now?" She answered her own question. "We wouldn't last long in the city. Couldn't afford to pay rent for one thing. And then what is there? Living in some Hoovertown? Squatting in a cold alley, begging for change? Getting laughed at by everyone who walks by?" Delores glared at Harper. "I won't do that. Not to my friends. That's why I had them all stay here. But now that Titan's gone, I don't know that we can. Lorden will run us off and we'll have nowhere to go at all."

Chance looked back at the aging freaks and old animals. They were a pathetic lot and he had ruined their chance of protecting themselves. He'd torn away the curtain and revealed the illusion and now they were doomed; unless he and his friends did something about it. "We could help you, you know," he explained. "You see, I am a man in possession of unique talents and equipment. I may have been using mankind's fear of the unknown in the same way that you have. I can utilize that fear again and scare away Lorden's men."

"It won't be Titan," Delores replied. "It won't be the same."

"Wait a second." Tiny Tim moved closer to Delores. "No offense, Delores, but this place is a bit of a dump. What's Lucky Leo Lorden want with it? Can't really make much dough in opening it up back again. Not when everyone just goes to the cinema for entertainment and no one's got two nickels to rub together."

That was a question that had been bothering Chance as well. "Perhaps he was intending to burn Pixie Park down for the insurance money?" Delores suggested. "Does it matter?"

"It does," Chance said. "If this was a purchase that didn't matter to him, he won't mind letting it go; either to preserve the lives of his men from a murderous ghost or because it simply isn't worth the trouble. In fact, he may be content to let you good people just live here, as tenants and caretakers. Maybe that's what he wants."

"No." Harper's voice was grim. He put his hands in his pockets and didn't meet anyone's gaze. "It ain't that. Men like Lucky Leo Lorden don't get by with letting things go. They don't spend money on something they don't care about. And if he can't make a cent off of Pixie Park, then there's only one reason why he bought the place." He glanced up and stared at Chance. "It's gotta be something personal."

That was a possibility Chance hadn't considered. He realized how little he knew about Lucky Leo Lorden. The future Brooklyn kingpin had started as a smalltime hood in Red Hook, bootlegging his way to a modest fortune back in the Twenties. He wasn't connected to any of the big outfits, not Schultz or Luciano or Lansky or any of them, but he did work for hire and began to acquire a modest power base. He wasn't Italian, Irish or a Jew as far as Chance knew, so he couldn't back up his criminal enterprises by relying on a common ethnicity. Instead, Lorden made up for it in pure viciousness. After the Depression hit, Lorden moved further into Brooklyn. His fortunes had grown even bigger and he moved from bootlegging to running countless rackets. Money from booze went to pay off the proper cops and keep politicians in his pockets. His soldiers kept the population loyal and terrified. They were heavily armed and not averse to shedding blood. Now Lucky Leo had purchased Pixie Park and Chance had no idea why.

Just then, a shout came down from the glass tower that topped the elephant hotel's painted palanquin. It was the tattooed man. He had slipped back up the watchtower and now was leaning down, shouting over the crackle of rain on the elephant hotel's tiles. "Delores!" he shouted. "Two cars coming! Packards! Real fancy automobiles!"

Chance knew as well as everyone else who that must be. "Lorden," he said.

"None other and he'll be here within the hour." Delores' voice was dark. She stared at Chance, her eyes cold. "You said you wanted to help. What's your angle, Chance?"

It was time for the reveal. Chance smiled a little. He couldn't help be a little dramatic. "Tell me, Miss Douglas, have you heard of the mysterious Green Ghost who has appeared in the papers? The emerald avenger who has all of gangland fouling their trousers in pure terror?" His grin grew. "Well, as you are to Titan the spectral elephant, so am I to the Green Ghost."

That made Delores pause. She looked at Tiny Tim. "Is that true?"

"Gospel," Tiny Tim agreed. "And the Green Ghost will arrive, to frighten off Lorden and keep you safe."

Now Delores seemed a little relieved. "Come inside, Mr. Chance," she said. "It took a great deal of preparation before Titan was ready to ride. Perhaps the Green Ghost requires a similar amount of set-up. We can help you with that." She glanced at the sky. "It's still dark; that will help too."

"Everything to set the stage," Chance agreed.

Delores turned and headed for the stairs. Tiny Tim and the other circus freaks followed her inside. Chance started for the stairs when Harper grabbed his shoulder. The chauffer was uneasy, his face pale and streaked with rain. "Boss," he said softly. "You sure about this? It ain't exactly our business and we suffered enough tonight. You sure you want go picking a fight with Lucky Leo Lorden?"

Chance was quick to answer. "I created the Green Ghost to protect the innocent; to finally do something with all my magical expertise besides wowing Broadway crowds. And these people, the natives of Pixie Park, are innocent. They have spent their lives being abused by the world, set in cages because they are different." He paused and came to a cold realization. "Now they refuse to play by the rules of the world that has spurned them. When I put on the mask of the Ghost, I do the very same." He narrowed his eyes. "They deserve protection, Joe. They deserve everything. Now are you with me?"

Harper just smiled back. "You even have to ask?"

"I don't think I do." Chance pointed to the door of the elephant hotel. "After you, my friend."

"Sure thing, boss." Harper headed up the stairs and Chance followed. It was time to plan. Lucky Leo Lorden was like a hungry dog with his mouth around a bone. He wasn't going to give up easily and he had armed men backing his play. Chance hoped that the Green Ghost would be enough to keep Pixie Park's residents safe. If not, then Chance was more than ready to take lives. Tiny Tim and Harper would help him. So would Delores and her friends. Chance steeled himself for battle. After all, no matter what, the show must go on.

Nearly an hour later, the two Packard automobiles drove in front of the elephant hotel. They were sleek black vehicles, their headlights blazing into the dim light and their windshield wipers hacking at the dying downpour. The doors of the cars slid open. Six men stepped out, all wearing a makeshift uniform of dark overcoats and fedoras. The last one opened the door and held out an umbrella as Lucky Leo Lorden, the boss, emerged onto the boardwalk. Chance watched it all from his hiding place, behind one of the legs of the elephant hotel. He was dressed and ready. They had finished the preparations, readying the costume and equipment just minutes before Lorden's convoy arrived. Now Chance crouched low and watched as Lorden took a step closer to the Elephant Hotel.

Lucky Leo Lorden was a powerfully built man. He had wide shoulders and thick arms. Lorden wore the same expensive overcoat, suit vest, and tie as his goons. His face was hidden by the brim of his fedora and it was lined and weathered. His hair was thin and plastered to his broad forehead. Lorden's hands were half-hidden by the sleeves of his trench coat. The fingers were completely covered with slightly shiny black leather gloves. He stood under the umbrella, a fat cigar smoldering in the corner of his mouth. Then he tossed the Cuban down and stamped on it, grinding the ash down into the boardwalk.

He raised his voice. "Delores!" he called. "Someone's running things here and I got a feeling it's you! Come on out here!" Chance wondered how exactly Lucky Leo knew who Delores Douglas was. But there was no time to question Lorden's knowledge. Lorden reached into his coat and withdrew a revolver. The handle of the gun, and Lorden's fingers, were still covered by the long sleeve of his overcoat. "Get out here, Delores. Get out here or I'll start throwing lead at that elephant. That wood don't look thick enough to stop a bullet."

The door opened. Chance bit his lip and waited. He watched as Delores Douglas stepped down the stairwells. She hopped over the bottom step, then walked over in front of Lorden and his gunmen. She put her hands on her hips and stared up at him. "Mr. Lorden," she said. "I suppose you know that we're living here. Now, I know you purchased Pixie Park and…"

"That I did, freak," Lorden replied. "My name's on the goddamn deed and I can do whatever I want to the place. If I want to light a match and burn it to the ground so I can warm myself in the glow, then I can do it. No one will stop me." He pointed down at Delores. "And I want you and all your sideshow friends gone before dawn."

"Where will we go?" Delores asked.

"To Hell, for all I care." Lorden leaned closer. "You know what they used to think about your kind, back in the old days? Called them children of the devil. Changelings left by fairies. Left them outside to starve before they were out of diapers. Maybe your parents should have done that to you, Delores. Spared you a lifetime of grief." He clutched his revolver. Behind him, his soldiers reached for their weapons. Chance saw sawed-off shotguns and automatic pistols glistening in the softly falling rain. Heavier guns must be waiting in the cars. "Now get your friends and get out."

Delores just stared at him. Chance could only imagine the fear that the little woman must be feeling but she didn't show it. Instead, she looked at Lorden's weathered face and cocked her head. "You know," she said. "You look a little familiar."

"Is that so?" Lorden demanded. "How the Hell would..?"

"I know you," Delores said. "Or knew you. A long time ago." She nodded. "Yeah. I know you, Lucky Leo. But you didn't used to go by that name. I think they called you…"

Lorden raised his hand. The revolver leveled at Delores. Lorden's jaws were clenched shut, his wrinkled face contorted by cold rage. Chance knew that he was enraged. He was going to kill Delores and then his boys would probably gun down every soul in Pixie Park. Chance couldn't let that happen. It was time for the Green Ghost to make his appearance.

Chance dug into his belt, hidden by his long, dark green cloak. He grabbed a steel cylinder, a smoke grenade, and popped the pin with one finger. Chance tossed it into the middle of Lorden's gunmen. The gas released with a gentle rush. It billowed out, forming a thick cloud around them. Delores took the opportunity to move back, towards the safety of the elephant hotel. Angry and confused shouts came from inside the smoke. Chance darted forward, getting into character as he neared the gangsters. The Green Ghost was ready.

He spoke, keeping his voice dark and full of cruel purpose. "Lucky Leo Lorden." Chance threw his voice, making it project from all angles. A ventriloquist had used to look after him when he was a boy and his parents were working on the stage. He knew the art well. "And all who follow his banner. You are not soldiers. You are not men. You are maggots, parasites seeking to drain the blood of the innocent. You bathe Brooklyn in red. Today, your souls will face a terrible and green justice."

His costume stood out in the smoke, emerging from the billowing clouds. His green cloak covered him. His face was a grim mask, with oval hoops flaring his nostrils and lips, black paint darkening his eyes and colored caps yellowing his teeth. It turned his feature into that of a living skull, covered with softly glowing paint and shadowed under his slouch hat. He wrapped his cloak around him, revealing just enough of the face to be terrifying. Chance looked into the eyes of Lorden's men. None of them were raising their guns. They just stood there, watching him with wide and terrified eyes. The Green Ghost's appearance and reputation were more than enough. Fear had won the battle before it even begun.

The Green Ghost advanced. "Flee!" he ordered. "Run from Pixie Park -- or the Green Ghost will drag your souls to Hell!"

"Ah no!" A pot-bellied enforcer stepped back and bumped into his friend. "I heard about this guy! Pulled Frank the Tank into a sewer and snapped his neck like a twig!" His pistol was forgotten in his hand. "And now he's gonna do the same to us!"

Chance knew that they were nearly panicked. All it would take was a little more showmanship from a familiar source. "And the Green Ghost is not alone," he said, making his voice emanate from further down the boardwalk. "Pixie Park has its own defender, unjustly murdered and returned to seek vengeance against the world of men!" His voice boomed, like he was a vaudeville announcer bringing out the next act. "Flee, mortal men. Flee from Titan; the phantom elephant of Coney Island!"

That was Harper's signal. From further down the pier, Harper drove the Rolls out from behind some old food stalls. He rolled the automobile into the center of the pier. Its headlights flashed over Lorden's gangsters, blinding them with sudden light. They looked at the automobile and then they knew true fear. Chance and his friends had worked feverishly to prepare the car. Titan's metal head, the tusks pointing out and the eyes still glowing electric blue, was lashed to the end of the hood. They had fixed smoke grenades below the headlights and along the runners. As the Rolls drove towards the packed crowd of hoodlums, it looked like the head of a might elephant was charging them while mounted on a body of living, billowing smoke. Harper was behind the wheel and he hurled a crackling

"The Green Ghost will drag your souls to Hell!"

string of firecrackers out the window. Sparks burst and made it sound like Titan was causing lightning as he stampeded towards his foes.

"Now run!" the Green Ghost cried. "Run and hold your souls close!"

He let his words linger as he faced Lorden's gangsters. It was working. They were edging back to their cars, eager to hop into the automobiles and speed far away from Pixie Park. But then Chance's eyes settled on Lorden. The kingpin's eyes were narrowed and quizzical. Chance's hopes began to fade. Lorden wasn't buying it. Suddenly, Chance knew why. It wasn't fear that was in Lorden's eyes, but curiosity; a professional curiosity. Like him, Lorden knew show business. When he saw a ghost, he wasn't fearing for his immortal soul. Instead, he was looking for the hidden wires.

Lorden pulled open the door of the nearest car. "Smoke and goddamn mirrors," he muttered. Lorden reached into the Packard and withdrew a Thompson submachine gun. Chance's heart pounded as Lorden swung the sub-gun around and took aim at the approaching Rolls Royce. "Don't be afraid of no spooks, boys!" Lorden cried. "Be afraid of me!" He leaned on the trigger and the Tommy gun started shooting.

A storm of lead ripped into the cloud of smoke. It cut across the smoky air over the boardwalk and tore into the front of the Rolls. Chance could only watch in horror as a good plan fell to pieces. The Thompson's rapid blaze of bullets cracked the windshield and shattered it. Glass flew through the air. Lorden kept shooting. He turned the gun on the hood of the Rolls. Bullets ripped into Titan's metal elephant head and cracked the hood of the car. Lead struck the engine. Chance knew that Harper was still in there, right in the center of those gunshots. Then the door of the Rolls slammed open. Harper hurled himself out scrambling from the seat. He struck the boardwalk and rolled. The Rolls blundered on, rolling past Harper on its cloud of smoke. It reached the end of the pier, crashed through the railing and then plummeted straight into the ocean. Chance heard the splash and saw bits of water rising as his car sank away for good.

Then Lorden turned his gun on Harper. "Trying to scare me, huh?" he asked. "You know what I've been through? You know the kind of horror I've seen?" He swung the muzzle of the Tommy gun to cover Harper, who still trying to pick himself off the pier. Chance couldn't let his friend die. It was time for the Green Ghost to act.

He kept an automatic pistol, along with a thin-bladed stiletto knife, in a special holster under his cloak. Chance pulled out the automatic and shot at Lorden. He never had been a good marksman. The bullet whined past Lorden's head, nearly clipping his ear. It didn't kill the Brooklyn crime lord, but it at least turned Lorden's attention away from Harper. Lorden turned and stared at Chance. He brought the Thompson to his shoulder.

"And you," he said. "The Green Ghost." He raised his voice. Around him, his goons had overcome their fear. They had just seen their boss send what was left of Titan crashing into the sea. Now fear was the furthest thing from their minds. They wanted to kill and Chance was straight in their sights. "All right, boys!" Lorden cried. "Let's show this fellow how we do things in Red Hook! Let's make sure that he's a goddamn ghost by the time we finish!"

There was no time to make another frightening tirade about the state of their immortal souls. Lorden's men were already reaching for their triggers. There wasn't even time to fire back. Instead, Chance broke into a run. He leapt through their ranks, running past the fading smoke as his coat billowed about like a pair of green wings. Lorden started to shoot and his six gunmen did the same. Bullets coursed around Chance. Shots tore at the fabric of his cloak. One punched through the brim of his slouch hat. Chance didn't have a plan. He just scrambled madly, racing away from Lorden and darting between the abandoned structures that stood before Pixie Park's main attractions. Chance glanced up and saw the Ferris wheel. Maybe, if he could get up high, he could slip away from Lorden. That might be his only chance.

He sprang behind a ticket booth and ducked down to catch his breath. Chance could hear heavy boots pounding on the creaking planks of the boardwalk; Lorden's soldiers coming in with their guns ready. Lorden's harsh voice cut through the silence. "We got him cornered!" he cried. "Keep firing and ventilate him and a grand to whoever shoots the bum first!" Chance gritted his teeth. At least he was leading Lorden away from his friends.

Chance drew his pistol, leaned out, and cracked off a few more shots. He fired blind, just enough to make Lorden's bruisers keep their heads down. The automatic cracked in his hands, hurling lead in the direction of his pursuers. Then Chance jammed the gun back into his holster and turned to run. He sprang away from the ticket booth and reached the bottom of the Ferris wheel. It loomed above him, a tall and skeletal figure of interlinked bars. Chance swung his arms back and forth, doing his best to limber up. After all the damage he'd suffered that night, a little more seemed almost not to matter.

A spring and a jump and he was in the air. Chance's firm arms caught the railing of the lowest gondola and then tensed and pulled. A lifetime as an acrobat served him well. He yanked himself and went flat on the roof of the gondola. It swayed back and forth under his weight like a vessel in stormy waters. Chance peered over the rim and looked down. Lorden and his men had followed him. They stood together under the Ferris wheel, staring at the ride with their cold eyes. Extra clips slammed into place and the weapons were reloaded and readied. Lorden walked closer to the Ferris wheel.

He stared up and this his eyes settled on the gondola. "There," Lorden said. "I can see a scrap of green." He pointed to the lowest gondola. "Go on," he ordered. "We got him pinned. Finish him!"

The phalanx of goons stepped under the Ferris wheel and raised their guns in a disorderly firing line. Chance rolled over, trying to make himself small. They started to fire. Bullets blazed into the gondola. It swung back and forth as sparks flew from the rusty metal. Shots cracked past Chance. Sooner or later, one would reach him. Then he'd be slowed and they could haul him down and make sure. He held his breath and looked around, searching in vain for some form of escape. Below him, the mobsters kept up their barrage.

Then one of them was shouting, louder than the gunfire. "Hey!" he said. "There's something under the Ferris wheel, right by that pillar, some kind of…" His voice broke off in a terrified scream. Chance peeked over the edge of the gondola and looked down. The two tigers, Benga's oversized pets, had charged out from under the Ferris wheel and pounced. The tigers struck down. The first tiger crashed onto a gangster and tackled him before sinking its fangs deep into the screaming man's throat. The other tiger lashed out with its claws, shredding a gunsel's belly before pulling him closer. Blood sprayed onto the boardwalk. Lorden and his men stood back in stunned silence, amazed by the brutal tiger attack.

Chance decided it was time to get their attention again. He leapt down from the top of the gondola and struck the ground with a practiced roll. The impact of the boardwalk against his shoulders and back felt like a cannon ball striking into his body but there was no time for the pain. Chance bounced back to his feet and kept running. Lorden and his four remaining henchmen followed, leaving the tigers and the two dying gangsters behind. Chance was growing tired and they were closing in. He looked around, searching for some cover. Behind him, the tigers roared and growled. At least they were getting fed.

Then Chance saw an old exhibit up ahead; a wide structure that had once been a display for unhealthy babies kept inside incubators. Exhibits like it had filled Coney Island in the old days, where passerby could stop and see the sickly infants kept alive by miracles of science. Now it was an empty structure, with a long counter set under a wide roof. The fading white paint and etched storks on the walls were fading away. Chance reached the counter and vaulted over it. He crouched down and rested there, drawing out his pistol as he heard footsteps and shouts coming closer. Lorden was down to four gunmen. He was far from being defeated.

More footsteps sounded over the boardwalk. They came from another angle. Chance looked up and saw Joe Harper, Tiny Tim, Terry and Delores Douglas scrambling through the door on the far side of the gallery. Harper had suffered a few bruises, but he was still on his feet with his automatic in his hand. They hurried over and crouched down next to Chance. Harper clutched his pistol and nodded to Chance, then pointed over at Lorden's men. Chance got the meaning.

They stood up together and opened fire. Their pistols thundered and sent a burst of bullets into Lorden's goons. Chance saw two of them go down, blood spraying from their overcoats and splashing over the planks of the pier. The bodies fell down, crashing hard on the wood. Chance wasn't sure whose shots had made the kills. He had a feeling it wasn't his.

"I'm out!" Harper cried. He ducked back and drew another clip from his pocket. Chance crouched down as well. Harper cursed as Lorden started shooting back. Shots blazed over the counter and tore into the wall behind them. Harper let out a little laugh. It grew into a mad cackle as he finished reloading his pistol.

Tiny Tim glared at him. "What's so funny, kid?" he asked.

"I wish I was a midget!" Harper laughed. "It'd make me a smaller target!"

"Wait." Chance raised a finger and Harper fell silent. The gunshots from Lorden and his soldiers had stopped. "They've stopped shooting," he said. "Do you think they'll..." Then he got his answer.

Lorden's voice bellowed. "Move, you dumb mugs!" he shouted. "Rush them; both of you!" His Tommy gun roared, laying down covering fire. Chance crouched low as the shots rushed over him. Then the remaining pair of mobsters raced across the boardwalk and reached the gallery. They arrived too fast. Harper hadn't finished reloading his pistol. It was up to Chance or they'd all be killed.

The first gangster reached the counter and leaned over, raising his pump-action shotgun. He swung the weapon down to cover Chance. Dodging the bullet was impossible so Chance did the next best thing. He grabbed the barrel of the shotgun and pushed. It pointed to the ceiling as the trigger was pulled. Lead belched out and cut a hole in the gallery's roof. Then Chance raised his own pistol. He rammed the muzzle of the automatic into the gangster's unshaven face and pulled the trigger twice. At that range, he couldn't miss. The pistol bucked and the goon's face shattered. He went down hard as brains sprayed on the fading paint.

Then the second of Lorden's boys came around the counter. He was closest to Tiny Tim and Delores and he raised his revolver and covered them. He was grinning at the midgets, like he couldn't believe that two people of that size would dare to stand against him. But Chance looked at Delores. He saw her splash some liquid into her mouth from a hip flask. Then she stood up, a match in her hands. She struck it on the wall of the gallery and held it before her mouth while her eyes, fierce and angry, focused on her attacker.

It made the gangster pause. "What the..?" he started and then Delores expelled a breath of blue fire from her mouth. Chance remembered instantly what Tiny Tim had mentioned about Delores Douglas. Her old act had been fire-eating. Now she was breathing out the flame and sending it straight into the mobster's face.

He reeled back. The smell of burning flesh filled the gallery. Chance watched as he dropped his gun and collapsed in a heap right at the feet of Lorden. Lucky Leo looked down at his screaming, writhing enforcer. Then his Thompson shot once and put a round through the man's skull, ending his screams for good. Lorden was alone now. He raised the Tommy gun, pointing it in the direction of the abandoned incubator gallery. Then he stepped back, moving cautiously and keeping his gun poised. After taking a few steps, he turned and ran. He dashed into the nearest building. Chance saw from the sign that it was the hall of mirrors.

Chance hauled himself over the counter. He holstered his pistol and drew the stiletto knife. "Stay here," he ordered. His good nature had drifted away in the firefight and now his voice was cold and direct. "I'm going to find him and finish him."

"George," Harper started. "He's got a chopper."

"And I'm the Green Ghost," Chance replied. "I'll finish him." He turned away and walked into the hall of mirrors.

It was dark inside, with bits of early morning sunlight poking in through holes in the roof. Chance looked around at the maze of funhouse mirrors as he walked inside. His image, the gaping skull and the misshapen face, was thrown back at him in a hundred different, terrible, and distorted ways. He had always hated the hall of mirrors. It was the one place where the audience became the show, where they were made hideous and deformed. Of course, for Tiny Tim, Delores, and the others, the world was like that all the time. Chance kept moving, holding his knife tightly. He heard other footsteps and followed them.

A magician knew how to move quietly as well as the value of misdirection. Chance glanced around the corner and then he saw Lorden, staring at his reflection in the circle of mirrors. Chance reached into his coat and withdrew a small, round bell. He hurled it into the center of the room. It rang crazily and made Lorden turn and fire. The Thompson blazed away as Chance moved. Bullets ripped into the mirrors and shattered them. Reflections came down in pieces. Lorden was shooting madly as Chance drew closer, wasting his shots on the reflections. Chance knew when to be still and when to move. He saw Lorden's terror, saw the fear in the kingpin's eyes, and then he closed in.

"Goddamn ghost!" Lorden swung the Thompson around. He rammed the muzzle into Chance's ribs and went for the trigger. "To bring me here! To this place! I'll teach you how you ought to treat me!" He moved for the trigger.

Chance's knife slashed out. It dragged along the length of Lorden's arm, slashing open his sleeve and drawing blood. Then it reached Lorden's hand and cut into his glove. Chance's other hand grabbed the fingers and twisted. Lorden screamed and stepped back. The glove came away in pieces and fell to the ground. Lorden's bare hand, clutching the Tommy gun, was finally visible. They both stared at it.

The hand was far from normal. It had two distorted fingers, both far too large. The tip of one was just small enough to fit into the trigger guard. Chance stepped back. Lorden clenched his teeth as blood trickled down his arms. The mirrors followed his expression of utter sadness and defeat.

A boot crunched on broken glass. Chance turned to see Harper, Delores and Tiny Tim coming inside. Harper had his pistol raised, covering Lorden. "Easy there," Harper said. "Just put the cannon down, Lorden. I don't want to waste you."

Delores looked at Lorden. "Leon," she said suddenly. "Leon the Lobster Boy."

"Yeah," Lorden said. "That's what they called me. I couldn't stand it, Delores. I couldn't stand the crowds and the laughter. I couldn't stand being a freak. So I ran away. I went to Red Hook and wore a set of special gloves everywhere I went. I made the world respect me." He clutched the Thompson and his finger moved for the trigger again. He started to raise the gun. "But this place was always there, nagging at me and reminding me of what I was. I needed to destroy it. I needed to wipe away everyone who had worked here and knew me as Leon. I needed to finally be free." He fired the gun.

The Tommy gun got a single round off before Harper's pistol barked twice. The shots crashed into Lorden's skull. His head snapped back and he slumped against the far well, then went still. Chance looked at his smoking gun. The Tommy gun hadn't hit any of his friends. Then Chance turned. He saw that the bullet had blasted across the room and struck the far mirror, putting a spider web of cracks into its center. The reflection in that mirror was still there though broken and changed somewhat. It showed Lorden. He had fired his last bullet into his own image and destroyed it.

Chance sighed deeply. It was over. He wiped the blood from his knife and sheathed it. "Well," he said. "It's finished." He looked back at Lorden. "He's finished."

"He hated the world," Tiny Tim explained. "But not as much as he hated himself."

"Come on," Delores said. "Let's get out of here."

They walked out of the hall of mirrors and back into the first lights of dawn.

A little later, after seeing to their various injuries, Chance and his friends said goodbye to Delores Douglas and the freaks. Delores and Benga took them to the edge of Pixie Park, back to the gap-toothed archway and the bridge that connected the boardwalk to Coney Island. Chance and Harper had a few bandages and all of them felt the need to sleep for a week. They would take a cab back to Manhattan, now that the Rolls Royce was under water.

Chance shook Delores's hand. "So, you and your people will be all right now?"

"Oh sure," Delores agreed. "Now that Lorden's gone, no one will have any interest in Pixie Park. We can keep on living like we used to. As for the dead bodies, we can get rid of those. There is the ocean, you know."

"And plenty of hungry animals to feed," Benga added.

Delores patted Tiny Tim's shoulder. "But you should come back, Timothy. Come to the elephant hotel and we can talk about the old days.

They weren't all bad, you know. We had each other."

"Yeah," Tiny Tim agreed. "That'd be swell."

"And Mr. Chance and Mr. Harper, you are welcome as well," Delores added.

"Wonderful," Chance agreed.

Harper seemed less enthusiastic. "Place still gives me the creeps," he admitted. "Even in daylight."

"Nonsense," Chance retorted. "It may have started out as a horrible place but Pixie Park has changed." He extended his hand to the old amusement park. "It has its residents and they have their lives; free and happy from the cruelties of the outside world. Mark my words, Joe. There are no ghosts here at all."

He turned away and walked back to Coney Island. Tiny Tim and Harper flanked him. They doffed their hats together to Delores and Pixie Park as they walked away into the warm morning sunshine.

THE END

SEEING THE ELEPHANT

I had never heard of the Green Ghost before Ron Fortier sent me a list of pulp characters that he was interested in, after I said that I'd like to try doing a short story for one of his anthologies. A lot of the characters seemed interesting but none really stuck out to me. Then I read about the Green Ghost and ideas for stories suddenly started springing to mind. A magician who fights crime with sleight of hand and reveals fraudulent ghosts like a 1930s Scooby-Doo? How cool is that? After I suggested the Green Ghost, Ron emailed me to explain that, fortuitously, he was looking for Green Ghost stories for an upcoming anthology. I thought about possible ideas for a day or so and soon came up with the story that you just read.

A lot of 'The Phantom Elephant of Coney Island' comes from fact as unbelievable as that may seem. Mr. Benga is based on Ota Benga, an African Pygmy who was taken from the Congo and was displayed alongside animals in the Bronx Zoo's monkey exhibit in 1906. Disgusting scientific racism kept Benga imprisoned until public pressure forced his release. He never overcame the cruelty and jibes of those around him and eventually committed suicide with a stolen pistol in 1915.

Titan's demise also based on fact. Topsy was a Coney Island elephant who lived at Luna Park and killed her abusive trainer. She was electrocuted as a spectacle devised by Thomas Edison as sort of a PR exercise to discredit Nikola Tesla's alternating current. Edison even had Topsy's death filmed. However, I'm unaware of there being any reports of her ghost.

The despicable Son-of-Ham shows and bizarre displays of babies in incubators are also real. There was an elephant-shaped hotel in Coney Island as well, which burned down in 1896. A lot of this story was inspired by Kevin Baker's *Dreamland*, which depicts all the squalor and sadness of turn-of-the-century New York and Coney Island.

I had always been interested in that era and the excess and strangeness of Dreamland, Luna Park and the other amusements of Coney Island. When I read about the Green Ghost's career in show business and magic, with a midget associate who was an old hand at performing, I knew that he would have to tangle with the more disreputable side of entertainment in his recent past. Sideshows and freaks must have been around George Chance even if he never exactly rubbed elbows with them. The strange dilemma of these people, forced to display themselves in order to make a living, seemed very interesting and I wanted to do a story that didn't make them misshapen villains or monsters, as would so often happen with pulp fiction of the time. I hope I succeeded.

Anyway, I hope you enjoyed reading this Green Ghost story. I'd like to thank Ron for giving me this chance and being a great supporter of my work. Getting to write this sort of story was something new for me and it was a big treat. Thanks again and keep an eye out for the Green Ghost. I'm sure his new adventures are far from over.

MICHAEL PANUSH – Only twenty-four years old, Michael Panush has distinguished himself as one of Sacramento's most promising young writers. Michael has published numerous short stories in a variety of e-zines including: AuroraWolf, Demon Minds, Fantastic Horror, Dark Fire Fiction, Aphelion, Horrorbound, Fantasy Gazetteer, Demonic Tome, Tiny Globule, and Defenestration. A graduate of UC Santa Cruz's Creative Writing program, he currently lives in Sacramento.

He has written several books with Curiosity Quills all of which are available digitally and in paperback. These include: *The Stein and Candle Detective Agency, Volume 1: American Nightmares, The Stein and Candle Detective Agency, Volume 2: Cold Wars,* and *the Stein and Candle Detective Agency, Volume 3: Red Reunion*: A collection of stories featuring the adventures of hardboiled private investigator Mort Candle and teenage occult genius Weatherby Stein as they solve arcane mysteries during the 1950s. *Dinosaur Jazz: Book 1 of the Jurassic Club Series*: A novel set on Acheron Island, a Lost World packed with dinosaurs, prehistoric beasts and mysterious ruins. At the height of the Roaring Twenties, Sir Edwin Crowe, the son of the explorer who discovered Acheron Island, must protect his home from the encroaching forces of modernization. *El Mosaico, Volume 1: Scarred Souls*: The first anthology about the adventures of Clayton Cane, a scarred bounty hunter in the Old West. Cane is a patchwork man, assembled from the body parts of Civil War soldiers and animated with mad science. He encounters monsters from Western legends in his violent quest for justice and peace.

He has also written a webcomic entitled, illustrated by Masmi Kiyono, which is available on the Curiosity Quills website at http://curiosityquills.com/looters-taking-tomes/

Please visit him at: http://curiosityquills.com/published-authors/michael-panush/) _

THE CASE OF THE ECTOPLASMIC ESCAPIST

Greg Hatcher

George Chance took a deep bow and said, "And now, ladies and gentlemen, before your very eyes I will…" He stopped in the middle of the grand gesture he was making and scowled, running a hand through his sandy blond hair. "No, that's not right. It doesn't look like Merry's toes are… it's just not working."

Merry White glared back up at Chance, but despite her scowl, there was a hint of wry amusement in her wide green eyes. "Well, I wish you'd make up your mind, darlin'. This isn't all that comfortable." A casual observer would have had to agree. Her head was poking out of a round hole in a red box. She pursed her lips and blew upwards in an effort to get her tousled mane of black hair out of her eyes. A pair of feet in sparkling golden slippers poked out of another hole. In a *different* red box, separated by about four feet from the one where Merry's head was frowning at Chance. The slippered toes wiggled as if to emphasize her words.

Chance grinned at Merry's exasperated expression, then shrugged. "No, let's forget it. Everybody out. This is too tame for the audience we're going to have at Bourdain's."

At Chance's words, Merry let out a sigh of relief and the hinged side of the box flew outward, revealing her cramped posture, legs drawn up to her chin. At the same time, the other red box opened, revealing Chance's old friend Tiny Tim Terry. The dwarf tore off the golden slippers with an explosive snort. "I thought it was humiliating working in the circus. But impersonating Merry's feet is some kind of career low point."

They were in Chance's residential brownstone on 54th Street, in the large basement area Chance called the 'rehearsal room.' This was where Chance worked to perfect the stage magic skills that had served him so well in his years of touring as a professional magician, and more recently in his new avocation: creating the persona of the Green Ghost, supernatural avenger of crime.

Chance shook his head ruefully. "It might turn out to be a career low point for me as well, Tim. I'm out of practice. I haven't performed for an audience, well, not for a *real* audience, scaring crooks doesn't count, in years. And to try a comeback in front of an audience full of fellow magicians and performers is the worst way to do it. They'll spot everything."

"Why'd you agree to it, then?" That was Merry, artless and direct as usual. She swung her feet to the floor, then stood and stretched her arms to the ceiling, trying to unclench her muscles from being curled up pretending to be sawed in half. In her practice leotard, Merry's tiny form almost looked like a toy ballerina atop a music box. Then she ruined the illusion by letting out a long whooshing sigh and plopping down on an old black steamer trunk. "Seriously. People have been begging you to come do shows for one charity or another ever since you retired and you always shut them down before they can finish the pitch. But these museum people, you didn't even put up a fight. Why this one?"

Chance thought for a moment, trying to frame an answer. "Because… I knew Barrett Bourdain. He was a mentor of mine, back in the old days. When he was still working the vaudeville circuit, doing an escape act. Simple stuff, straitjackets and handcuffs. Nothing like…" He shook his head. "I was there that night in Edgarton, you know. I was in town, you remember, Tim, it was a couple of years ago, after we wrapped up that business with the Gravens poisoning. You and Merry had come back here to New York but I stayed an extra night. I wanted to see Barry's new show and I thought maybe we would have a drink after or something, I was going to surprise him."

"What? The museum…it's *that* Bourdain? The guy that burned up?" Merry was horrified.

"Yes." Chance's voice took on an edge. "And you see? That's the first thing you think of with the name Barrett Bourdain. 'The guy that burned up.' That's why I couldn't refuse. I don't want Barry Bourdain's name just to be known as the escape artist who fumbled his act and died." He jabbed a finger at Merry, who shrank back a little at Chance's emphatic tone. "Barry was *brilliant*. He was an accomplished stage performer, and a gifted escapist. He showed me everything I know about how to slip handcuffs, how to pop a straitjacket; the things he taught me have saved my life as the Ghost countless times. Yours too, for that matter," he added. "What's more, Barrett exposed dozens of supernatural fakers and con artists. He did more to discredit the fake psychic industry than anyone else, before or since. He was a magician's magician. There was no one on earth better prepared or more knowledgeable. There's no earthly reason why he should have died that night." Chance fell silent, scowling.

Tiny Tim ran a hand through his thinning gray hair and pulled out a cigar, but at a fierce shake of the head from Merry, reluctantly put it back in his shirt pocket. He pulled up a small step-stool and sat. "What did happen that night, boss?"

"I still don't know." Chance shook his head. "He had done the Flaming Coffin a thousand times, all over the country. It was a combination escape and vanish, simple stuff really. It was just the fire that made it a spectacle."

Seeing Merry and Tim's bewildered expressions, he went on to explain, "Barry worked it like this. There'd be a wooden cabinet, upright, and he'd be hanging upside down from a hook at the top, straitjacketed, cuffed, and padlocked in. He'd get someone from the audience to come up and take a look, the whole thing. Really sell it. But the cabinet had a hidden hinged back, so the whole back side opened like a door and a metal base with a secret drawer where the keys were. Once Barry had popped the straitjacket, he could reach down with his cuffed hands and get the key and slip the whole cuff-and-chain mess with no problem, and while the assistant was spinning the thing around, showing the audience all sides, he'd already be loose. Then, as they'd drape the cabinet with a cloth, Barry would open the back and step out and away. That left the cabinet. The cloth was actually draped over a tiny wire frame, invisible to the audience, and open at the back, so the cloth was draped over the wire, not the cabinet itself. Once Barry was out, while the assistant did a little patter and the band played, he'd lift the cabinet carefully out, off of the base, and slide it backstage, with the cloth on the frame hiding him from the audience. Then the assistant would set the cloth drape on fire. It was treated to go up in a sheet of white flame, like flash paper. So the fire goes whoosh and suddenly there's Barry, in his tux, stepping forward out of the floating ashes. To the audience it looked like the coffin had caught fire and disappeared, leaving Barry free with no evidence of chains, cuffs or straitjacket. It was a showstopper."

"Sounds like," Merry said, admiringly. She had been Chance's onstage assistant when he was touring and could appreciate the skill and ingenuity of such a trick. "That's even better than the aquarium gimmick. And faster too."

"So how did it go wrong?" Tiny Tim asked.

"No one knows," Chance said. "The show was going well. I was in the back, enjoying the spectacle the same as everyone else. Barry was in fine form. Everything went the same as it always did. Then the buildup for the Flaming Coffin, the business with tying him up and hanging him by his heels in the cabinet and so on. Even when you knew it by heart, and I did, it was still a good show. Except this time, the fire just blazed up and kept going… and just as we were starting to think it was taking too long, the blaze collapsed all over the stage, flaming bits of the cabinet everywhere. We could *smell* it; wood smoke and kerosene and burning meat. The cabinet was still in there, and so was Barry. Still jacketed and cuffed… and burned to a cinder. Martha Abbott, his assistant, just about had a breakdown. She thought she'd killed him. Because it was her job to light the fire, you see."

Merry looked ill. Even Tiny Tim turned a little pale.

Chance looked up at the others, a little bleakly. "Sorry. It was a terrible thing. You know, the things we do are dangerous. Certainly I've taken risks on stage and even bigger risks now, as the Ghost. There's always the chance something will go wrong. It's part of the profession. But…not like that." He paused, again. "You do everything to can to insure there will be no problem. I even do it as the Ghost, leading crooks into traps and things I've set up in advance. You *prepare*. Always. Always check it, and check it again. Barry taught me that." He scowled.

"That's why you took the job," Merry said suddenly. "You think someone murdered him."

"It was ruled accidental." Chance smiled a thin, wintry smile. "But yes. I think it was murder. I was too shocked at the time to really see it clearly, but I've had a lot of time to think about it since then. I don't think it was Martha," he added hastily. "The poor dear has never gotten over it. That's why she and her husband Jim have worked so hard the last couple of years to put the Bourdain Museum Foundation together, it's atonement for them. Jim was Barry's manager and agent and Martha was his onstage assistant. They both loved Barry."

"Then who?" Merry wanted to know.

"I don't know. It's all just guesswork." Chance shook his head grimly. "But I think *someone* killed him. The easiest way would have been to sabotage the straitjacket; use one of the modern ones that can't be slipped, leaving Barry trapped. There's no way to tell until you're actually in one and your shoulders can't move. If that's the way it was done, the subtlety of somehow sabotaging the Great Bourdain's signature illusion and making him die on stage; that's the kind of criminal showmanship that almost certainly points to a fellow magician or stage performer of some kind. And the only ones that knew the secret of the Flaming Coffin were Barry, the Abbotts… and those of us that Barry mentored. Fellow magicians. I'm guessing the killer's one of those other magicians, and whoever that is, he's probably going to be in the crowd invited to the opening this weekend."

"So it *is* a case for the Green Ghost after all." Merry looked triumphant.

"I suppose it is." Chance shrugged. "But we still have to put a show together by the weekend, either way. So let's get back to it, shall we?"

Later that day, Chance sat down in the upstairs drawing room with the other two members of his team, Glenn Saunders and Joe Harper, to brief them about the Bourdain Museum's opening gala. "This is going to be a bit more of a challenge for the Ghost," he told them. "The place is going to be full of magicians and stage people, and they'll know all my tricks. These are smart, skeptical professionals trained in creating illusions, so the usual superstitions that help the Green Ghost along won't be in play at all. That's why I want to keep you two in reserve. But some of them have used doubles as well, so you'll have to be on your guard especially, Glenn."

Glenn Saunders nodded. He could have been George Chance's twin brother, but in truth he had chosen to largely abandon his own identity a few years back in order to substitute for Chance at need. Glenn had thought this a good bargain in return for Chance's rescue of him from homelessness and poverty, at the height of the Depression, and he had never regretted the choice.

Chance had spotted Glenn on a park bench and noted the already-amazing resemblance. He promptly offered Glenn an apprenticeship and a steady paycheck, in return for doubling Chance on stage once in a while. A little plastic surgery cleaned up the few niggling differences, and after that it was impossible to tell the two men apart. Later, when Chance embarked on his nocturnal crusade, Glenn Saunders had proven to be an invaluable alibi for the Green Ghost many times. For his part, Glenn had just been happy to be working, and he soon found a reborn sense of mission and self-worth aiding Chance in his quest. For a man that had literally forsaken his own identity in favor of another's, he was remarkably contented with the hand life had dealt him, and the person he had become.

Glenn raised an eyebrow at Chance's words. "How long do I have to fool them? Hours? Days? Should I be studying up on these birds? Are they good friends of yours?"

"Not *good* friends, no." Chance smiled. "More like friendly rivals. The competition. I was thinking I might need you to do the evening show, though, while the Green Ghost prowls around and sees what there is to see."

Saunders brightened at this. Chance was tutoring him in stage magic, it was part of their bargain, but Glenn rarely got to really practice his craft in front of an audience. "Great!" His face fell. "Shouldn't we be rehearsing?"

Chance winced a little. "We should," he admitted. "The trouble is I don't know what show we're doing yet. We'll have to put our heads together with Merry and Tim." He shook his head. "Time enough to hash all that out before the weekend. Joe, I have a job for you as well."

Joe Harper's reaction was the opposite of Glenn's. He grimaced and said, "I shoulda known. Here I was thinking the non-magician guy of the group would get the weekend off."

Glenn snorted. "Yes, you need a rest from your hard week of loafing and playing the ponies. And burning the eyes of innocent passers-by."

"You talking about my outfit?" Joe looked wounded and tugged at the collar of his green-and-yellow plaid blazer. Coupled with his red bow tie and white straw boater hat, it was an ensemble that probably could have been spotted from a passing airplane three miles up. And for Joe Harper, it was subtle. "This is *fashion*."

Chance ignored this byplay and went on, "Joe, while we're at the mansion, I'd like you to poke around the town a bit. See if you can get a line on what folks thought of Barry Bourdain. Murder isn't random. There has to be *something*, some reason a killer wanted him dead. Someone in Edgarton knows what it is. Let's find out who."

Joe nodded. "Sounds good. Talking to people is what I do best." He grinned. "Don't suppose I get an allowance for buying them drinks, maybe."

Chance smiled and held up a finger. "A *small* one. I want information, remember."

"Information always comes easier with a little lubricant, you know that." Joe grew serious. "Only... I don't know where I'd start to get a wedge in. You gotta gimme something so I can figure an angle. What kind of guy was this Bourdain, boss?"

"I was wondering that too," Glenn put in. "You seem, I don't know, a little knotted up about this one, chief."

"Perhaps a little." Chance's smile was rueful. "Maybe it goes back to what I was saying before. Magicians don't usually have friends who are also in the business, there's always an undercurrent of rivalry. But Barry Bourdain was my friend. When I saw him die on that stage, I was so shocked... it seemed so impossible... I just froze. And then the place was swarming with police and people from the coroner's office and of course there were all the newshounds." His expression grew distant, and regretful. "It gnaws at me that I forgot what Barry taught me. *I got rattled.* I didn't keep my head. And as a result, I may have missed my opportunity to get his killer." He straightened, trying to shake off the bleakness that had again momentarily overtaken him. "I owe Barry. That's all. This is my opportunity to make it right."

"Chance's second chance." Joe grinned. "I like it. So tell us about Bourdain."

Chance considered it. "He was… brilliant is the word I keep coming back to. Not just as a magician, but at everything. Nothing ever seemed difficult for him. It led to an attitude that some may have thought of as arrogant, but for Barry it was just the certainty that he was the smartest man in the room. He usually was right." He sighed. "He didn't lord it over people or anything like that, but he was impatient with those who couldn't keep up. It's possible he made enemies. But mortal enemies? Someone who would kill him in such a spectacular way? I can't think of anyone who hated him that much. That's your angle, Joe. Find out what might trigger that kind of hate."

Joe Harper snorted. "Hell, I don't have to go snooping for that." Two fingers went up. "First, money. Second, a woman. Period. It's one or the other. Or maybe a woman with money. Or a woman what needs money. But it's one of them two things."

Glenn asked, "Did Bourdain have a girl?"

"Many. None serious." Chance thought a minute. "You may be on to something though, Joe. Maybe there was a woman somewhere in the background. It's a place to start."

"Just playing the percentages." Joe shrugged. "It's what *I'd* bet on."

"All right. Off with you, then. Tomorrow and Thursday we rehearse, Glenn, I promise. Then you two take the roadster and find a hotel in Edgarton Friday morning. Merry, Tim and I will drive up in the Rolls later that day. We'll be at the museum."

"Wait, it's a hotel, too?" Joe raised an eyebrow. "Fancy."

"The museum is actually Bourdain's own mansion," Chance explained. "The Abbotts have spent the last year and a half converting it. The ground floor is all exhibits and a small performance stage, but the upper floors are still residential, the Abbotts live there now. They're putting us performers up there for the weekend, as well."

Glenn looked like he was about to say something, then paused.

Chance spotted the hesitation. "What, Glenn?"

"Well…." Glenn's expression grew dubious. "Chief, I know you ruled them out, but don't these Abbotts have the best motive of anyone for wanting Bourdain dead? It seems like they got the most out of it, if they were the heirs. They live in the mansion, they trade on his name…."

"Business heirs only." For a moment Chance's voice sharpened, then he realized that Glenn had a perfectly valid point. "Sorry, didn't mean to snap. But remember, I was *there* that night; I saw Martha's face when Barry died. It's simply not possible she had anything to do with it. And Jim Abbott was here in the city, on business. The police checked him out first thing. He was alibi'd for the night of the performance, and the following morning, by several different witnesses." He shook his head. "And anyway, neither Jim nor Martha is the kind of extreme personality that would commit a murder as flamboyant as the one we're talking about. Our killer's a showman, I'm certain of it." Suddenly, Chance grinned, but there was no humor in his eyes, only icy resolve. "Fortunately, so am I. And I have a plan for an unscheduled performance from the Green Ghost that should smoke him out. I hope so, anyway."

The Bourdain mansion, now the Bourdain Museum, was a huge Gothic castle of a place, just north of Edgarton, off Route 22 headed toward the Hudson Valley. It squatted like a great scowling stone toad on an acre of lawn, surrounded by thick woods on three sides.

"Nice digs," Merry said, as Chance pulled up to the main entrance in the big green Rolls. "Only thing missing is the moat and a couple of archers stationed in the turrets."

"Barry did actually consider a moat when he was building the place," Chance replied. "Couldn't figure out a cost-effective way to divert water up here though. There's a stream over a little ways beyond those trees." He pointed. "It disappointed him. His original idea was to build a full-on miniature castle, including a moat with a drawbridge and a walled-in courtyard. He liked the medieval look."

"I think he got it, even without the moat." Tiny Tim pulled out a cigar and lit it. Merry wrinkled her nose in distaste. Tim noticed and said defensively, "Hey, I waited till he stopped the car."

"You couldn't have waited until we were out?" Merry shook her head and stepped out of the car onto the gravel driveway.

As Chance and Tiny Tim followed, the main doors swung open and a woman in a gray dress appeared. "George! How lovely to see you! And Tim, you old reprobate." She knelt and gave the dwarf a hug, then stood and faced Chance and Merry. "George, thank you again for doing this. It means a lot."

"For you, anything, Martha." Chance nodded at Merry. "Merry, this is Martha Abbott. Martha, my assistant, Merry White."

Martha Abbott still looked good, Chance noted. She'd kept her figure and, if his math was right, she was still barely on the sunny side of fifty. It was only when you got close that you could see the lines on her careworn face, and a couple of thin streaks of gray in her auburn hair. "Come in and meet the others," she said. "It's quite the gathering."

They followed her up the steps and into the foyer. Inside, just past the vestibule, there was a large open area with a marble floor and several exhibits on stands, most of them under glass. Props from Bourdain's magic act; handcuffs, a top hat, and on one large display stand against the far wall, a padlocked straitjacket mounted on the headless torso of a mannequin. Milling around among these displays were a variety of elegantly dressed people, many of whom were holding drinks.

"I feel way underdressed all of a sudden," Merry said, looking ruefully down at her blouse and jeans. "I didn't think the party was till tonight."

"Nonsense," Martha Abbott replied. "You've had a long drive, no one expected you to arrive in evening wear. Would you like to run upstairs to your room and freshen up?" At Merry's fervent nod, she clapped her hands. "Haddock, come help Mr. Chance and his friends with their luggage."

A tall, cadaverously thin man trotted up to the group and, after Chance handed him the keys to the Rolls, disappeared out the front door. Tim followed, muttering something about finishing his cigar in peace. That left Merry and Chance standing in the foyer. "Can I show you to your rooms?" Martha asked them.

"You go ahead, Merry." Chance glanced over Martha Abbott's shoulder and suddenly straightened. "I'll follow you two in a moment. I'd like to say hello to some old friends."

The two women went over to the stairs at the edge of the foyer, while Chance started back to where the other guests were talking and laughing. Almost before he entered the room, a young man in a white dinner jacket bumped into him. He looked around rather wildly. "George Chance? You *are* George Chance, aren't you?"

"I am." Chance blinked. "And you are?"

"I'm Blake Anthony," the young man said, and added hopefully, "The Amazing Anthony? Youngest magician to tour the United States and Europe as a solo?"

"Ah. Well, I haven't really kept up…" Chance was saved from the awkward moment by the approach of a portly fellow, resplendent in a

"I'm Blake Anthony. The Amazing Anthony!"

black tuxedo and a maroon bow tie. He had a luxuriant black beard and a mustache that had been waxed to needle points. "Hello there, Grayson. How have you been?"

"Well enough," wheezed Grayson. "I see you've met the junior member of our little fraternity. I hope you aren't bothering Chance with your ridiculous theories, Anthony." He clapped Anthony on the shoulder with enough force that it verged on assault. The young man staggered a little. "It's one thing when it's small talk amongst ourselves, but Chance has become something of a celebrity crime-solver, friends with the police commissioner and all that. How is that going Chance? See you in the papers every so often, you must be doing well out of it, eh? Have to be if it lured you off the stage. Well, good for you, I say. I could never let it go, though; the lure of the boards is too great." Grayson thrust his thumbs into his lapels, elbows out, addressing an imaginary audience. "Ladies and gentlemen, before your very eyes..."

"...we shall disappear," Chance said hastily. "Sorry, but I've got to say hello to Jim Abbott, I saw him there in the back." He drew away before Grayson could protest.

Blake Anthony followed, anxiously. "Mr. Chance, I really did want to speak with you..."

Chance ignored him, pushing through the other guests towards a stooped, white-haired man with a bushy beard. "Jim? How are you?"

Jim Abbott glanced up, visibly brightening as he saw Chance approach. "George! Bless you for coming. You look great. It would have made Barry so proud, seeing you today. Is Tim with you?"

"He's out front, helping your man with the luggage."

Abbott chuckled. "Smoking one of his foul cigars, no doubt." The chuckle turned into a cough. "Sorry. Got a bit of a cold. Shaking too many hands, I guess. Spent yesterday at a town council meeting, getting all the permissions we need to do business here in the county. My voice is shot."

"Well, it must have been worth it. The place looks amazing. It really is a museum." Chance gestured at the various displays. "A lot of work went into this."

"Yes, well." Jim Abbott ducked his head, embarrassed.

Chance nodded at the straitjacket display. "I saw you had this old jacket mounted and had to come see for myself. This is the one we all practiced in, right? With the extra-long right sleeve and the pocket?"

"Yes indeed." Now there was warmth and humor in Abbott's raspy voice. "All you boys put in your time in that smelly old thing. You, Grayson, even Cheng Kim..."

"What? Kim's here?"

"We tried to get everyone," Abbott said. "We wanted everyone who had apprenticed with Barry. You know Cheng is still doing that ridiculous 'Oriental mystery' tour, even with the way things have been going with Japan and China in the news lately. He's not even really Asian, did you know that?"

"I did. He told me he was actually from Houston. His father was an oil wildcatter and his mother was a singer in a *cantina* just south of the border." Chance smiled at the memory. "He used to say that meant showbiz was in his blood. I think he finally made the name change legal. It was too hard to get promoters to cut a check to Alberto Davis after 'Cheng Kim' had wrapped a show. And we all called him Cheng, anyway."

"Well, he's here and still sporting that absurd pigtail." Abbott snorted. "I don't think he's come downstairs yet but certainly you'll see him at dinner." He stiffened. "Oh, Lord, it's that Anthony kid again, it looks like he's about to accost Martha. Forgive me, George, I have to go."

Chance nodded, amused. Jim Abbott shouldered past him towards the front vestibule where Blake Anthony was gesticulating fervently at Martha Abbott.

Merry appeared at Chance's elbow, looking very sophisticated in a seafoam-green cocktail dress. Chance eyed the dress with a small smile of approval. "Green. Good choice."

"When you're on the clock, fly the colors." Merry smiled mischievously. "You did say we were here on the Ghost's business."

"I did. And now I'm sure of it." Chance pointed at the straitjacket mounted in the glass display box. "Take a look."

Merry obediently inspected the display, then shook her head. "I guess I don't get it, darlin'."

"That's Barrett Bourdain's stage straitjacket. The one that's rigged with extra give in the right sleeve and a key pocket sewn into the chest. I recognize it. All of us practiced in it, it smelled like an old sock." Chance grimaced. "The thing is Barry was allegedly wearing it when he died. It should have burned up."

"Then how..."

"Exactly," Chance said. "Jim just confirmed it's not a replica. I don't think he realized what I was getting at but Martha worked with Barry on stage every night for years. She *has* to know that this wasn't the jacket he was using on stage the night of his death."

Merry's eyes grew wide. "No wonder she looks so nervous. She..."

"...knows that Barry was murdered," Chance finished. "Yes. And she's covered it up. For two years. I wonder why?"

"Maybe the Ghost ought to ask her," Merry said.

"Tonight," Chance nodded. "Slide away when you get a chance and call Glenn at the hotel. We're going to need him here sooner than I planned. Back lawn, eleven o'clock tonight. Tell him to wear the tux."

Merry raised her hand in a mock salute. "As you command, my liege," she said, and departed.

Chance watched her go, then turned back to the straitjacket display. It wasn't proof, not hard evidence, nothing that would stand up in court. *There's no reason in the world why Bourdain couldn't have two rigged straitjackets*, was the first thing a policeman would say. But Chance was sure. This confirmed it was murder.

"Mr. Chance, I really need to talk to you." It was Blake Anthony again. "It's about Barrett Bourdain and the night he died. You were there, weren't you?"

"I was." Chance's smile was a little strained now. The boy meant well and his earnestness was hard to dislike, but he was going to be a nuisance if this kept up.

"Then you know he was murdered."

That got Chance's attention. Was Blake Anthony on to the straitjacket as well? Was that what he was trying to talk to Martha Abbott about a few minutes ago? "What makes you say that, young man?"

"Because he's haunting this place. He can't rest until his killer is caught." The young man's voice grew urgent. "You have to understand; I've *seen* him. Walking the grounds. Last night."

"You saw the ghost of Barry Bourdain." Chance's patience was at an end. His voice dripped with sarcasm. "I don't know what you're trying to pull, but you picked the wrong crowd. The people in this room have seen every kind of hoax and fake..."

"It's *not* a hoax," Anthony said, desperation edging his voice. "I can't sleep; sometimes going for a walk relaxes me. I saw Bourdain on the lawn last night at midnight. I *know* it was him. Christ, his picture's all over the place in here, it'd be impossible not to recognize him. I'm not setting up a stage gimmick or rigging anything, that's not my act at all. I do cards and hand work. Ask anyone. I'd never soil his memory with a cheap publicity stunt. *I saw his ghost.* Please, you've got to believe me."

Anthony's voice had taken on the ragged hoarseness of someone near tears. Chance relented. "All right. I believe you saw *something*." He shrugged. "But even if you did... why come to me? Why not the Abbotts, or..."

"Because you're the expert." Blake Anthony dropped his voice to a whisper. "Because I know you're the Green Ghost. This is what you do."

Now he *really* had Chance's attention.

At roughly the same time George Chance was trying to frame a reply to young Blake Anthony, Joe Harper was standing in an alley behind a bar in the town of Edgarton, staring down the barrel of a gun, and trying very hard not to let his expression show the fear he was feeling.

"Let's try again, showboat," the man holding the gun said. His voice was laconic, almost bored. "You been asking questions. A *lot* of questions. About stuff people don't want to talk about. It's making folks nervous. This is a nice quiet town. You should be nice and quiet too."

"You know, the gun's really not necessary," Joe said. He could feel sweat beading on his forehead. "I didn't realize there was a taboo or something. I just like talking to people. I heard about the fire and I was curious, that's all. It ain't a crime."

"Naw." The man with the gun was not impressed. "You like to talk, yeah. But liking to talk about one night two years ago? At three different watering holes? That ain't liking to talk. That's what cops do."

"For God's sake." Joe was honestly offended. "Do I *look* like a cop?"

"No cop I ever met dressed like you, that's for sure." The gunman eyed Joe and his ensemble. Today's was relatively understated, a white-and-maroon checked jacket over a pink shirt, with a gray tweed cap and a bow tie that was the blazing red-orange of a Tahitian sunset. "But you're too nosy. Shamus maybe. Something."

"I just like hearing a good story," Joe protested.

The gun jerked up.

Joe instantly raised his hands and said, "Okay, fine. I'm a writer. A book writer. Researching, that's all. I thought maybe I would do a book called *The Strange Death of Barry Bourdain,* something like that."

The gunman actually blinked. "Bourdain? But…"

There was a muffled explosion and the alley filled with green smoke. Harper let out a squawk. There was a moment of scuffle and when the smoke cleared, suddenly another man was there, holding the .45 he had plucked from the gunman's hand.

"Allakazam," Glenn Saunders said, pleasantly. "And for my next trick…"

The gunman stared in astonishment at Glenn and Joe for a moment, then he broke and ran.

Glenn started after him, but Joe laid a hand on his arm. "Forget him.

I don't think he knows enough for us to risk getting perforated over. He might have friends. What'd you find out?"

"Not as much as you, obviously. You sure got somebody stirred up." Glenn scowled. "Damn it, Joe, that guy might have led us to something that would have cracked this thing."

"Or just to us getting our heads cracked for good." Joe waved it off. "Anyway, I think I got something good already."

Glenn brightened at this. "Give."

"Well, first of all," Joe said, "Edgarton ain't the sleepy little place you'd think it was. Back during Prohibition, it was the biggest clearinghouse for Canadian liquor in the whole state. There was just one guy that ran the whole shebang, name of Raintree, and he ran it the way Mussolini runs his trains. Anybody got out of line, they got themselves croaked. Then after Repeal, he just disappeared."

"Disappeared? What do you mean, disappeared?"

"I mean vanished. Gone. Allakazam, not there." Joe shrugged. "One day he was there, the next day he wasn't. Maybe he ran. Maybe he retired. Maybe he got sick and died. No one knows. But everybody *is* sure that he left behind a big stash of dough."

Glenn considered it. "Okay, but what's that got to do with..."

"Getting there. Be patient, young man." Joe grinned at him, enjoying the moment. "Here's the good part. The night Raintree did his fade *is the same night Barry Bourdain was killed.*"

Glenn whistled. "Okay, you win. That is something good."

"Gets better. There was another fire that same night, at Raintree's old warehouse. Whole place went up like the Fourth of July." Joe jabbed a finger at Glenn. "Put it all together and see if you get what I got."

"Huh." Glenn's brow furrowed. "Bourdain was tied up with Raintree. Raintree decides to run, whatever reason, doesn't matter, the heat's on. So he torches the warehouse and kills Bourdain. Cleaning up as he goes." He paused. "But what the hell would Raintree want with Bourdain in the first place?"

"It's adorable, the way you trust in the goodness of people." Joe gave Glenn a pitying look. "You look at Barry Bourdain and see a famous stage magician. But if you're a bootlegger looking to move illegal hooch, what do you see? You see a guy with a free pass to travel all over the country with a bunch of odd-sized boxes with all kinds of hidden compartments in them. For God's sake, you've had the boss teaching you how to hide stuff in boxes like that for three-four years now. Bourdain had a huge entourage, it was a caravan. What better delivery driver could you have, if you want to transport illegal goods all over the east coast?"

"Okay." Glenn nodded. "I get it. But…" He shook his head. "Say you're right. Two years ago Raintree killed Bourdain and ran. If that's so, we've got no place to go from there. He's disappeared. You said so."

Joe Harper nodded. "I thought so too, kid, till our friend with the gun showed up. So *somebody* in Edgarton still has a hand in it somewhere." His face fell. "I got no idea who, though," he admitted. "Or why."

"The *money.*" Glenn snapped his fingers. "The stash you were talking about. That's got to be it. He's still looking for the money. Bourdain must have moved it. Hidden it somewhere. Raintree killed him too soon!" He clapped Harper on the shoulder. "C'mon, we gotta go tell the chief."

Joe looked nervously around. "Suits me. I'd just as soon get off the street. I'm feeling like a real target now."

"Maybe you shouldn't dress like one then."

"This is my *undercover* outfit!"

Glenn just shook his head. The two men set off at a trot back to their hotel.

Night had fallen, turning the shadowed woods surrounding the Bourdain estate into something black and sinister.

George Chance, looking very elegant in a black tuxedo, opened the French doors leading to the balcony from the lavish upstairs dining room, and stepped outside onto the flagstone walkway. There was a good view of the back lawn from this second-floor vantage point, and Chance strode to the parapet and leaned forward, squinting. *Yes. There.* He glanced quickly over his shoulder at the dining room where he could see the other guests talking and laughing. In particular, he was looking for Blake Anthony. Chance smiled when he saw that Merry and Tiny Tim had engaged the young man in an animated conversation… in such a way as to maneuver him so that Anthony had no view at all of the doors or the balcony beyond.

No moon. Good. Chance nodded and checked his watch. 10:58. *Right on schedule.* Then he placed both hands on the stone parapet and flipped himself over the wall.

Most men attempting such a feat would have been writhing on the ground with a broken ankle, but George Chance was the son of a trapeze artist, raised in a circus; for him this was no different than going down the back steps. He twisted in mid-air and his heels struck the top of the hand-carved granite arch over the entrance to the downstairs gift shop.

The granite only extended out from the wall by five inches or so, but that was more than enough for Chance to perch for a moment, drop to a catlike crouch, and then spring out and down to land silently on the soft green lawn below. Thankfully, there were no lights here like those overlooking the front drive to the museum, and Chance in his tuxedo was just one more black shadow among the others on the lawn. He set out at a lope, across the lawn, to the woods at the rear of the estate.

As he reached the trees, Glenn Saunders stepped forward, dressed in an identical black tuxedo. "Here you go," he said, and handed Chance a small leather valise. "Packed light, like you said. Just the usual Ghost gear, nothing fancy."

"Good." Chance took the valise and opened it, pulling out a long, bottle-green duster. He shrugged out of the tuxedo's dinner jacket and into the duster, tugging loose his tie as he did so. He pulled the lapels of the long coat close and then tucked a scarf, also dark green, over the remainder of the white shirt front the duster's lapel flaps had left visible. Then he knelt and pulled a small makeup kit out of the valise and set to work on his own face, working by memory and feel. Once this was done, Chance lifted out a prosthetic jaw piece and fit it over his lower face, then stood and turned to face Glenn. "The hat?"

"Oh. Here." Glenn handed the transformed Chance a large black slouch hat. "Sorry. I just never expect you to be so quick."

"Practice." Chance tugged it over his ears and then, finally, thrust a small stickpin into the scarf around his neck. He reached into the duster's left pocket and felt for a small plastic box with a switch, and thumbed it on. A tiny hidden lamp in the stickpin lit his face with lurid green light.

Glenn Saunders suppressed a gasp. He had seen this transformation hundreds of times, but it still spooked him a little. George Chance was gone, replaced by the eerie, skull-faced figure of the Green Ghost. There were deep black pits under the eyes, distended nostrils like those on a mummified corpse, and an exposed bone jaw that leered at Glenn Saunders with a frozen skeletal grin. The tiny lamp made it look like this grotesque visage was softly glowing green.

"Okay?"

"You mean terrifying?" Saunders replied. "Hell yes."

"Good." The Ghost nodded and thumbed the switch off, returning his face to shadow. "Your job is Blake Anthony. He's the fellow I told you about on the phone this afternoon. You and Merry and Tim keep him busy and, especially, away from the guest rooms."

Saunders nodded. "Gotcha. Since I'm you, is there anything you need me to know about this afternoon? Specifically? I already know all the faces, I think, and can put names to them."

"Just that Anthony thinks I'm the Ghost. I pooh-poohed it and brushed him off, but I don't think he bought it. It doesn't matter as long as he's with you. With me, I mean. If he's with 'George Chance,' he won't be stumbling around trying to catch the Green Ghost at work."

"Okay. Heading back in." Saunders eyed the balcony doubtfully. "I think I better use the door, though."

"Down's easier than up, certainly." The Green Ghost chuckled. "I just didn't want to cross the dining room floor with Anthony watching my every move. But I wouldn't expect you to climb the wall. Tim taped the downstairs doorjamb before dinner, so the entrance is open and going in that way won't trigger any alarm. Peel the tape after."

Glenn nodded. "And you?"

The Ghost glanced up at the house. "I think I'm going to have a look around the Abbotts' rooms. I want to know if Martha and Jim knew about Barry and this man Raintree.... And what Raintree's got on them that kept them silent, if they did."

"What about the ghost of Barry Bourdain that the Anthony kid was going on about?"

The Green Ghost snorted, and despite the green jaw mask Saunders could hear the wry smile in his voice. "If he exists at all, he'd have to be..." Suddenly the masked figure stiffened. "Oh, for God's sake. I am an *idiot.*"

"What is it, chief?" Saunders was a little taken aback at the vehemence in his employer's tone.

"...Straitjackets," the Ghost said, softly. "By God. Anthony was right. There really *is* a ghost haunting this place."

"I don't get it."

"I don't either. Not yet. But I will, after the Ghost has a quiet word with Martha Abbott." The voice had turned hard and grim.

"But I thought you said the Abbotts were in the clear," Glenn said. The *I told you so* was left unspoken.

"I still think they are. At least, for murder. But Martha's been lying to all of us. I want to know what she's afraid of. " The Ghost's tone was curt. "Until I know that, we won't know what to do next. So clear the way for me to find out. Head up to the house before George Chance is missed. Watch Anthony. And tell Merry and Tim to try to keep Jim Abbott busy." And with that, the Ghost faded into the darkness.

"There really is a ghost haunting this place."

Not very far from where the Ghost had been speaking to Glenn Saunders, there was a somewhat overgrown dirt track leading through the woods, its route roughly following the creek that bordered the Bourdain estate before eventually snaking back out on to Route Twenty-Two. At the bend of the road that was closest to the Bourdain property, Joe Harper stood leaning against the side of Chance's roadster, wondering how long it had been since he had dropped Glenn off. The agreement had been to wait half an hour in case there were new instructions from the Ghost, but so far there had been just the forest noises.

The great outdoors was not Joe's favorite place, especially the forest at night. The quiet murmur of the creek was soothing, but Harper did not feel soothed. The afternoon's encounter with the gunman had rattled him more than he wanted to admit, and anyway these woods were just damn spooky. *Why, between the dark and the crickets and the creek, a fella could sneak right up on...*

A twig snapped a few yards off and Harper started, violently. He fumbled his pistol out of his jacket pocket and brandished it, knowing it was futile to try and aim at anything given the shadows on this moonless night, but holding the gun made him feel marginally less vulnerable. "Glenn? Boss?"

No answer. Just a vague rustle or was it the creek? Harper leaned forward, holding his breath.

The rustle came again, unmistakable this time. Harper snapped, "Who's there? Come out where I can see you!"

Suddenly there was a great crunching and snapping of twigs, and Harper could discern movement in the trees; whoever it was had decided to run. Harper's teeth bared in an unconscious snarl. *Enough of this mysterious crap. I didn't chase the last guy, but by damn I'm chasing this one.* He bolted after the fleeing shadowy figure.

The pursuit was awkward and clumsy, *the blind chasing the blind*, Harper thought ruefully. He could barely see enough to keep his footing. His quarry seemed to be heading deeper into the woods, away from the road but at a tangent to the Bourdain mansion. Certainly he knew his way better than Joe did. Harper was never going to catch him at this rate, clumsily picking his way through the trees the way he was. He decided to chance breaking into a run and promptly tripped over a protruding tree root. Joe's head slammed painfully into the trunk of the tree and he spun and fell, spitting a string of oaths as he tumbled headlong into a tangle of ivy and ferns.

As he fell, he thought he heard an odd sound. A faraway, keening whine. But then it was gone, and Joe decided he must have imagined it. For a moment he just lay there, cursing his idiocy. *Well, that's torn it. No catching the son of a bitch now.* Harper sat up, feeling a mixture of foolishness at his attempt at pursuit and relief that none of his friends had been there to see it. He brushed pine needles off his jacket and sighed. *At least,* he thought, *it's got to have been half an hour.*

Painfully, Harper struggled to his feet and looked around, suddenly realizing he had no idea which way led back to the car. He could barely see three feet in any direction, and in the blackness, the trees all looked the same. The fall and subsequent roll through the bushes had completely disoriented him.

Harper muttered another weary oath. *Lost in the woods. Never going to hear the end of that. Swear to God this is the last time I go chasing off after something without any idea what I'm getting into.* All right, the dirt track ran parallel to the creek, so, if he listened for the creek that should eventually take him to where the roadster was parked. It wasn't much of a plan, but it beat waiting for sunrise. *At least try to be more careful where you put your feet,* he told himself.

He paused, listening for the sound of the stream. Yes! There it was… behind and to his left. Slowly, Harper moved toward it. He had progressed perhaps ten or twelve feet when he heard another series of noises. These were coming from behind him. A series of crashes, a scream… and gunshots.

That's Glenn. Or the boss. Or both.

It had to be happening at the Bourdain estate. Forgetting his resolve of only a moment ago to be more careful, Joe Harper stumbled as best he could through the trees towards the sounds of chaos coming from the estate.

At the mansion, the informal cocktail party that had sprung up after dinner was beginning to wind down as the various guest magicians and the members of their respective entourages excused themselves to go to bed. The dining room still had quite a few people in it, but the tone was less boisterous as conversations were becoming muted.

With one exception. At the table where Chance and his crew had been sitting, Blake Anthony showed no sign of fatigue, somewhat to the chagrin of Tim and Merry. "So you really never suspected? Not at all?"

Merry rolled her eyes. "I didn't suspect because it's not *true*. George consults with the commissioner on cases sometimes because he's interested and he likes puzzles. But that's all there is to it. Your idea that he's this Green Ghost guy? I really just can't figure it."

Anthony leaned forward, eager to expound. "Look. The Ghost has to be a magician, or at least someone who knows stage magic. The police reports are practically a list of every kind of stage vanish there is. He goes up in a puff of smoke, he mysteriously disappears from rooms where all the exits are covered or locked, he's all about illusion and misdirection. So there's that. Then there's the showmanship, dressing up like a glowing green ghoul like he's a character out of a Republic serial. He's clearly a trained escapist since handcuffs and chains mean nothing to him, lots of crooks have testified to that."

Tiny Tim snorted. "So? That's half the guys in this room. Including you, probably."

"Yes, but..." Anthony dropped his voice to a lower tone and glanced around. "George Chance retired from touring a little over three years ago, and that's almost exactly when the Green Ghost first started to appear. They're both in New York. They've been involved in the same cases quite a few times..."

"Aren't you forgetting the part where we've been seen at the same time? By numerous witnesses?" It was Glenn Saunders, doing his very best George Chance impression. Merry marveled at how good he had gotten; it wasn't just the voice, but also the insouciant delivery, the casually elegant posture. "I told you before, young man, you're barking up the wrong tree."

"Supposing that's so, you've at least *worked* with the Ghost, right?" Anthony didn't look convinced. "Maybe you even trained him."

"I've seen him." Saunders' voice was patiently polite. "Our paths have crossed. But that's all. He's a vigilante, Mr. Anthony, operating outside the law. I could never condone that."

"But his methods...the stage magic..."

"My dear fellow." Glenn waved a hand around the room. "This room is full of people expert in stage magic. Did I train them all? No. Why should it follow that I must have trained this Green Ghost, then, just because he uses tricks we know? Be reasonable."

Anthony shook his head in frustration. "That's not..."

"Oh, let it go, Blake." Merry turned her most dazzling smile on him. "You're spoiling the party. Why don't we go find another martini?"

"No, thanks," Anthony said. "I might as well go to bed. I think I might even be able to sleep tonight. Good night, all of you. Sorry for any, uh..."

"Forget it." Saunders smiled. "I don't actually mind. It's a bit flattering.

But I just can't see myself running around on rooftops dressed like the Phantom of the Opera."

Anthony nodded, a little uncertainly, and walked off. When he was out of earshot, Tim muttered, "Well, we shook him, anyway. But damn he's stubborn."

"And smart." Glenn sighed. "I almost feel bad misleading him; he really did do a nice job of putting the pieces together. I hope he's done for the night, I don't think I've ever had anyone watching me that closely when I'm doubling the boss. Sooner or later he'd have tripped me up." He glanced around the room. "And he's the only one here that hasn't known George Chance for years. I doubt I'd last even that long with any of these others. Usually I just have to be seen. I'm not an actor."

"Yes you are, you're doing great," Merry assured him. "Anyway, it's not for much longer. Everybody's tired. I think it's getting to be bedtime even for us show folk."

"Anything for us from the chief?" Tim wanted to know.

"Keep Anthony out of his hair. And watch the Abbotts." Glenn looked around the room again. "Where are they, anyway?"

"I think they went upstairs to bed," Merry offered. "So really it should be safe for us to call it a night, too..." She sat up straight at a noise from outside. "Wait, was that a shot?"

There were three more bangs in sharp succession, then a splintering crash from above.

"What the hell?" Tim stood on the seat of his chair to get a better view of the French doors and the balcony beyond. "Did someone just go out the window?"

"Let's find out," Glenn said, and the three of them moved toward the doors to the patio.

A few minutes earlier, Martha Abbott had entered her bedroom and reached for the light switch when she heard a whispered hiss.

"Leave it off."

She looked up, startled, and saw a shadowed figure with its back to the glass doors that led to the widow's walk overlooking the dining-room patio. Suddenly the face was lit with a soft green glow and she gasped in horror as she saw the corpselike face of a ghoul looking at her from under a black slouch hat.

"I mean you no harm," the Ghost said in a harsh whisper. "Where is your husband?"

"He's locking up," Martha Abbot said. "But he'll be here soon, I promise you. Don't think you'll..."

"I said I meant no harm." The Ghost's whisper held a note of reassurance. "Do you know who I am?"

"The Green Ghost." Martha Abbott's voice shook a little, then steadied. "Blake Anthony was talking about you today. He thinks you're a stage magician, George Chance. I know that's not true, but... who are you? Why are you here? You don't scare me in that getup," she added.

"I'm someone interested in Barry Bourdain." The Ghost's whisper sharpened. "And in why you have been lying about his death."

The Ghost's outfit might not have shaken her, but his words did. "I'm not...." Martha's voice trailed off. She sat heavily on the bed. "How did you know?"

"The display below. The straitjacket. I have surveillance on your hall and I heard your husband talking about it."

"I don't..."

"It *smelled*," the Ghost snapped, out of patience. He had to break her before Jim Abbott came up. "Everyone who spoke of it, all those who apprenticed with Bourdain, they all said that it stank like old gym socks, no matter how many times it was laundered. You would have known instantly that it was the wrong jacket as soon as you were buckling Bourdain into it and *so would Bourdain*. It would have immediately put him on his guard, especially if he feared an attempt on his life."

Martha made a sound that was something between a sob and a sigh. "How much do you know?"

"I know Barrett Bourdain is not dead. And that he's hiding here, somewhere. I know that he was running a smuggling operation. I know about Raintree and the warehouse fire. What I don't know is if you were in on it with him all along."

Martha Abbott just shook her head.

The Ghost went on, relentlessly. "Since there was a burned body, *someone* was killed... and that makes you an accessory to murder. Who *really* died on the stage that night? Why would you cooperate with a hoax like that? Were you and Bourdain having an affair? Does your husband know?"

"My husb..." Abruptly Martha Abbott seemed to gather herself. "Leave my husband out of this!"

"Then tell the truth," the Ghost rasped. "Quickly, before he walks in on us."

"All right." Martha took a deep breath and went on, "You have to know I had no idea anyone would die. Barry needed to disappear. He and I… we had been… together, occasionally. It had ended, but he trusted me enough to enlist my help. We found him a double for the show that night, an out-of-work actor who resembled Barry well enough, but we couldn't rehearse him properly, so Barry needed to be on hand. They switched halfway through the show; we thought he could manage the Flaming Coffin with Barry to help him, so the actor was the one that went in. But… something went wrong. The cabinet must have been sabotaged. Then there were the police and the coroner and it was so crazy… and Barry was gone. I thought he was dead too."

"But now he's back."

"Yes." Martha gave a shuddering sigh. "He came up to me, disguised, at the grocery store a few weeks ago. He said it was time to stop running. He wanted to try and set a trap for whoever had rigged the Flaming Coffin to go wrong. Only the apprentices and I knew the secret, Jim didn't even know it. So we set up this weekend…. Barry was sure one of these magicians was working with Raintree. He was going to try and expose him. But you're here now, talking about Barry and me as accessories to murder. You'll ruin everything."

The Ghost ignored her plea. "Where is Bourdain now?"

"He's hidden in the sm…"

The bedroom door flew open. "Who's in here?" Jim Abbott roared. He was holding a deer rifle and instantly aimed it at the Ghost. "So help me, if you've hurt my wife I'll…"

Then everything happened at once. The Ghost hurled a pellet to the floor that exploded in green smoke. Jim Abbott fired the rifle, cocked it, and fired again. The Ghost spun away but felt a hot red spike punch through his upper arm. Desperately, he lashed out with a booted foot at the doors behind him. The glass shattered and the Ghost dived through the opening, two more rifle shots following as Jim Abbott fired blindly through the roiling smoke. Clumsily, with none of the grace George Chance had exhibited an hour before, the Green Ghost tumbled from the upper balcony to the patio a floor below, outside the dining room, landing with a painful grunt on the flagstones. Clutching his wounded arm, the Ghost ducked out of sight under the widow's walk just as Jim Abbott emerged, coughing, and leaned out over the railing above him. "Martha! Call the police!"

Lights started coming on, illuminating the dining room patio and the back lawn. Beneath the Green Ghost's prosthetic jaw, George Chance grimaced. *This just gets better and better.*

He looked around and saw there was an area of the patio still in shadow. *There's my exit.* The Ghost ran for the parapet and vaulted over, gambling on a lifetime's training to land safely. Fortunately, there was nothing below at that point but lawn and the Ghost managed a reasonable tuck-and-roll on to the soft grass. He got to his feet and took off at a staggering run for the woods just as Merry, Glenn, and Tim burst through the French doors from the dining room. Merry shrieked as she saw Jim Abbott on the balcony above raise his rifle and fire one more time. It was enough to throw Abbott off his aim, and by then the fleeing figure of the Ghost had disappeared into the trees.

"We have to help him!" Merry said in an urgent whisper. "He looks hurt!"

"I think Joe's still out there." Glenn's face looked white and drawn in the faint light coming from the dining room. "I hope so." A new realization straightened his shoulders and his eyes grew wide. "Jesus Christ, if he's hurt then I'm going to have to keep on being George Chance the rest of the weekend."

"Both of you, pull it together." This was Tiny Tim. "You want to help, do your damn jobs. Right now, that means we're George Chance and his friends and we don't know nothing. Cops will probably…"

There was a shout from below. It was Haddock, the butler. "There's a dead body!"

"Oh God!" Merry rushed to the parapet. The other two followed.

Below, they could see Haddock standing over a motionless figure lying face-down on the lawn. Merry sucked in her breath sharply and Glenn laid a hand on her arm. "Easy. It's not him. Look again. No hat, no duster."

More lights came on. They could see Jim Abbott emerge out on to the lawn just as Haddock rolled the body over. It was Blake Anthony.

"Blake!" Merry gasped. "But who would…?"

Glenn clamped down harder on Merry's arm just as Martha Abbott came through the French doors behind them.

Martha walked slowly to the parapet where they were standing and said, "Police are on their way." Her voice shaking, she added, "It was the Green Ghost. He was here. It must have been him. He's a murderer."

It was only five-thirty in the morning and so far, it was already shaping up to be the worst day of Glenn Saunders' new life.

He had no idea whether Chance was alive or dead. None of them had gotten any sleep. Merry and Tim were both clearly agitated and wanted to be out searching for their wounded chief, but the police had cordoned off the estate, no one in or out, and they had forbidden the houseguests even to use the phone so there was no way to check in with Joe Harper. Moreover, Glenn had to stay in character as George Chance all the time, with no break of any kind because the police had herded them all into the dining room and insisted they wait there, and he was dreading the moment when Grayson or Kim or the Abbotts would come up to him to make small talk. He had studied their biographies before coming to Edgarton, and Chance had coached him a little... but Glenn knew that it still would be a minefield to navigate even a simple conversation with any of these people, most of whom had known Chance for years.

Remember to keep Chance's posture and body language. Use Chance's facial expressions showing fatigue and annoyance, not his own. Fidget as Chance. Even just sitting at the table in the Bourdain dining room, there were a thousand tiny details Glenn had to remember or the whole masquerade would collapse.

And then there was Inspector Ludgate, who was proving to be the most difficult obstacle of all.

Ludgate was the senior law officer that had been dispatched to the Bourdain mansion, a walrus-like man in a bowler hat who clearly took a dim view of show people in general and magicians in particular. Glenn and Tim and Merry were seated at one of the large round tables with Grayson and Cheng Kim, and Ludgate was standing over them, scowling. "I still am not clear on the sequence of events," he said. "Blake was here in the dining room with all of you. He said he was going upstairs. Then there's the shouting and the shooting, and Abbott chases this Ghost character out of the bedroom where he falls out the window and then jumps off the patio. The Ghost runs off into the woods and suddenly there's Anthony, dead on the lawn. Is that it?"

"That's it." Tiny Tim glared up at the inspector and lit a cigar. For once, Merry didn't make a face at him over it, but just sat, staring out the window at a couple of uniformed officers that were out on the lawn.

"For God's sake," Grayson burst out. "How many times must they recount it for you? There was a prowler. Anthony must have surprised him on the way in and this Green Ghoul chap did for him then. Then Abbott chased him out with a couple of shots from his deer rifle. Wounded him, by all accounts. Why aren't your men out there combing the woods for him?"

"They are." Ludgate was unmoved by Grayson's exasperation. "But that story doesn't make any sense. A prowler who's surprised in the act, surprised and desperate enough to murder, does one of two things. Flees the scene or hides the body. This one did neither. I'm not convinced he had anything to do with Anthony's death at all."

Cheng Kim leaned forward. He was a tall, ascetic-looking man with deeply tanned skin and veiled black eyes. His hands were hidden in the voluminous red-and-gold sleeves of his satin kimono. His long black hair was woven into a pigtail that Glenn estimated was almost two feet long. His voice was sibilant, almost a whisper. He was playing the part of the mysterious Oriental to the hilt, and it was difficult to remember that Chance had said he was really from Texas. "Then you suspect one of us?"

"I think it's possible the killer is still on the grounds here, yes." Ludgate looked at the group with disapproval. "Or that the Ghost had a confederate here in the house."

Kim smiled thinly. "What motive would any of us have had for killing young Anthony? We are a small but closely-knit fraternity, Inspector. Many of us apprenticed to Bourdain, in the old vaudeville days."

"Most murders happen within families. And motive can be as simple as a moment of anger. Show people are noted for their intemperate behavior." Ludgate waved it away. "Motive will reveal itself when we catch the person who did it. Right now my concern is *how* it was done. The sequence you've all described doesn't make any sense. Anthony's supposed to be up on the third floor in his bedroom but instead he's dead on the lawn of a broken neck. Did he fall? My forensics guy says no. Anthony was out on the lawn and someone came up from behind and just twisted his neck and broke it the way a farmer does a chicken for Sunday dinner. That's someone big, someone with tremendous upper-body strength."

Tiny Tim said wryly, "Well, that lets *me* out."

"Not entirely." Ludgate smiled, but there was no humor in it. "An inspection of the downstairs entrance in the rear, facing the lawn, shows a fragment of tape on the doorjamb. Like someone had taped over the tongue of the lock. That suggests to me that the prowler had a confederate inside the house."

Glenn kept his face very still. Inwardly, he thanked God that he had safely flushed the wad of tape down the toilet that he had removed on his way in. He was chagrined that he'd apparently left a tiny piece though. *Check it and check it again,* he reminded himself. *Damn it anyway.*

"A confederate to do what?" Merry couldn't hold it in any longer. "You are so wrong! About everything! We've seen the Green Ghost at work, down in Manhattan. He's not a murderer! Call Commissioner Standish, he could tell you…"

"*Enough*, Merry," Glenn snapped, in Chance's most authoritarian tone.

Ludgate regarded them all expressionlessly. "I'll want to talk to you all later, one at a time," he said. "Mr. Chance? A word?" He indicated the doors to the outside patio.

"Certainly," Glenn said with an enthusiasm he did not feel at all, and followed the inspector outside. "What can I do for you?"

Ludgate regarded Glenn for a long moment. It was an old trick, Glenn knew; remain silent, try to rattle the other person into blurting something out just to end an awkward silence. Glenn admitted to himself that he was rattled, but this small-town cop was going to have to do better than that. He raised a quizzical eyebrow, just as George Chance would have done, and drawled, "Well? We do have a show tonight, Inspector, so I hope we can wrap this up soon."

"Yes." Ludgate nodded. "The show. Who's it for?"

Glenn blinked. "Why anyone who wants to come, I suppose."

Ludgate took off his bowler hat and sighed. "Well, that's the trouble, Mr. Chance. See, Jim Abbott told me he was talking to the town council about the business license for this here concern, but so far that hasn't been issued. So his grand opening here can't really happen yet." He spread his hands. "But you all are putting on a big show. You can't charge for it. It's not even been advertised. But everybody says the Abbotts set it up weeks ago. So who's it for?"

Glenn was as mystified as Ludgate. He said the first fully truthful thing he'd said to anyone since the police arrived. "I have no idea, Inspector." He shrugged. "Probably they just forgot about the license. But really, I'm just a featured performer, not the promoter. I'd ask the Abbotts." He turned to go.

"One more thing." Ludgate's tone sharpened.

Glenn halted and turned to face the policeman. "Yes?"

"Why was Blake Anthony so obsessed with you?" Ludgate's eyes narrowed. "Everyone I've spoken to, even the servants, say that Anthony followed you all over the place last night, harangued you with questions, asked everyone else about you and your history. What was he driving at?"

"Oh, that." Glenn let out an amused chuckle. "He thought I was the Green Ghost. Obviously, *that's* been disproven."

"Obviously." Ludgate let it hang for another long, awkward moment.

"...I hope we can wrap this up soon."

Glenn continued to regard him with his best approximation of George Chance's lazy half-smile.

Finally Ludgate harrumphed and said, "Tell me about the Green Ghost. You've seen him? Met him? In New York?"

"He's involved himself in cases that I consulted on with Commissioner Standish. I've seen him in action. I wouldn't say that I've *met* him." Glenn Saunders had never had tried so hard to sound casual… but not *too* casual, not like a liar. *And you're Chance,* he reminded himself. *Speak as Chance.*

"What's his interest? Why would he be here?"

"I don't know." Glenn spread his hands. "I truly don't. I can tell you that I don't believe the Green Ghost is a wanton murderer. I understand that he has killed, but only when shooting it out with gangsters or something like that. I can't see him killing someone as harmless as Blake Anthony."

"Unless Anthony was a threat to him somehow."

"Pfft." Glenn waved it away. "The Ghost concerns himself with criminals. Anthony and his conspiracy theories didn't even rise to the level of an inconvenience. You should know he was equally convinced that the ghost of Barry Bourdain was haunting the estate." Another Chance-esque chuckle. "Dotty. Anyway, if the lad was inconveniencing anyone, it was me."

Glenn regretted it the second it was out of his mouth and inwardly he raged at himself for falling into the inspector's trap. *Never mind. Ride it out. Your alibi is solid, in the dining room in front of a dozen witnesses. He knows it.*

"Yes. So you and others have said." Ludgate let it hang again, waiting.

Glenn smiled and said, "Look here, Ludgate, I'd like to help. Perhaps we could join forces. I've had some success assisting the police in New York…"

"We roll our own upstate, Mr. Chance. But thank you."

"Very well, then. But you shouldn't hesitate to call on me." Glenn smiled, politely, and decided it was his turn to let it hang.

Finally, Ludgate turned and stepped back into the dining room. "We'll be speaking again, Mr. Chance."

Glenn nodded, hoping the smile he was wearing didn't look as pasted-on as it felt. "Looking forward to it. I hope to hear news of an arrest soon."

As Ludgate returned to the dining room, Merry and Tim brushed past him to join Glenn out on the patio. As soon as the doors closed behind Ludgate, Merry clutched at Glenn's sleeve. "What was *that* all about?"

"Fencing match." Glenn let out a long, shaky sigh. "God. I think I better claim a migraine or something and go hide out in the bedroom. I'm never going to be able to keep this masquerade up all day."

Tiny Tim made a noise somewhere between a snort and a grunt. "You're doing fine, kid. But we need to get hold of Joe somehow, find out…"

"Nix," Merry hissed. "Shut it." She nodded at the French doors, which were opening again.

Cheng Kim emerged on to the patio, his pace so steady that he appeared to be gliding above the flagstones. His red-gold kimono looked resplendent in the morning sun. "I trust you have not been unduly inconvenienced by the inspector."

Glenn shrugged. "He's just doing his job."

"Yes. We all have our work to do." Kim's voice was soft, and he glanced around before adding, "I have known Tim for many years and I know that he would never be party to murder. Certainly I did not wish to create difficulty for you three with the police." Now Kim looked directly at Glenn. "But I must know. Who are you, and where is my old friend George Chance?"

Chance came awake slowly, only aware of the pain in his upper right arm at first, a hot throb that pulsed with his heartbeat. He reached across his chest with his left hand, trying to feel out the damage, and his fingers touched bandages.

"Hey, boss?" Joe Harper's voice, tentative and nervous. "How you feeling?"

"Been… better." Chance opened his eyes. "What happened? Where are we?"

"At the hotel." Harper's relief was a palpable thing. "Been out most of the day. You caught one in the shoulder getting out of Bourdain's. If you didn't wake up soon I was getting ready to say the hell with the Ghost and get a doctor up here somehow." His long, horsey face split in a shaky smile. "You lost a lot of blood."

"Jim Abbott got me with his deer rifle." Chance smiled weakly in return. "Good thing he uses a light load. If he'd had a thirty-aught-six or a shotgun I'd really be a ghost now." He raised an eyebrow. "Lucky you were there."

"Luck hell." Joe snorted. "I went to go see what all the ruckus was about. I'd dropped Glenn off and was waiting around in case you had something for me, like we planned, and then I heard someone else in the woods out there with me. I went after him, but I lost him, and then the shooting started, so that's where I went. Found you passed out at the edge of the woods, bleeding like a stuck pig, so I got you back to the car and lit a shuck." Harper grimaced. "Hell of a time getting you up here. Thought I was going to have to dig a bullet out of you. But it looks like it went clean through. Ruined a bunch of hotel towels getting you patched up, got you out of the Ghost gear and stashed it, and here we are."

Chance was reminded again that Joe Harper had the heart of a lion, despite his avowed laziness and his carnival barker's fashion sense. Quickly, he sketched the evening's events for him, finishing with, "… and then Abbott kicked in the door and started shooting. He must have heard my voice and thought I was a burglar." He paused. "Thanks, Joe. I mean it. You really saved my bacon."

"Cash bonuses always welcome." Harper flashed a crooked grin, then grew serious. "Boss, there's more. You missed them by inches but cops were swarming the place by the time I got the car back out on to Route 22. Radio this morning said there'd been a killing up there."

"A killing!" Chance struggled to sit up. "Merry and Tim…Glenn…"

"All fine," Harper told him. "Far as I know. No, the guy that got himself croaked was some kid named Anthony. That's all they said. Cops are working on it."

"Blake Anthony's dead?" Chance fell back on to the pillows. "But that doesn't…"

"Doesn't make any sense?" Harper spread his hands. "What's new? None of this business does. Seriously, look at it. What the Abbott dame told you was crazy. That's no kind of plan. Substitute an actor and then run? How many years did you practice to do what you do? Why put some out-of-work actor on the spot like that, draw so much attention to the substitute? You want to decoy somebody, you don't put all eyes on a stage where you *are,* you want them looking where you're *not.*" He let out a sigh of disgust. "The best way to hide something is to hide it. The best way to run is to run. This convoluted…"

Chance held up a hand. "Wait. 'The best way to…' good God, Joe. You've cracked it."

"Huh?" Harper looked pleased, then baffled. "Cracked what now?"

"I mean I know who killed Blake Anthony. And Barry Bourdain."

"But I thought you said Bourdain wasn't dead?"

"I did." Chance grinned, then frowned. "But our killer definitely has two murders to his credit. Bourdain's and Anthony's. The trouble is I have no idea how to prove it." He struggled to sit up. "Come on, help me get dressed. We've got to…"

"Hey, whoa there, tiger, you just woke up," Harper protested. "Don't you think we oughtta at least check in with Merry and Tim, let you get some rest? Glenn can do the show tonight, you guys rehearsed. If it ain't canceled."

"I'm surprised at you, Joe. The show must go on. You know that." Chance grinned. "And now it's got a whole new third act. But you're right, we need to get Tim and Glenn and Merry."

The telephone rang, startling both of them.

Harper picked it up. "Hello? Tim? Yeah, he's here, seems fine. Jesus Christ yes we were worried. Cops said no phones till now? But then what are you...wait, what?" He blinked, and then handed the phone to Chance. "Says he's got someone wants to talk to you."

Chance nodded and put the receiver to his ear. "Hello?"

"George? My friend?" It was the soft tones of Cheng Kim.

Chance's vision swam for a second. Had Glenn been exposed? What the hell was this? "Uh..."

"It is all right." Kim's voice held reassurance. "Your secrets are safe; we are calling from Merry's room. No one can hear. And we have known each other many years, you can trust me. After speaking for some time with Tim and Merry, and also with this extraordinary young man who wears your face, I am persuaded that we should not work at cross purposes." He paused. "I have a secret too, my old friend. I am no longer just a touring magician. I have another job.... with the Treasury Department."

Chance absorbed this information and then the realization hit him. "Raintree," he said. "You want Raintree and his smuggling operation. It's still in business, isn't it? Repeal didn't slow them down at all. They just diversified their services."

"We think so, yes." Kim's voice was becoming clipped now, leaning more towards the G-man than the Oriental wizard. "Hashish, opium, perhaps even women from Siam and India. The network operates all along the Eastern seaboard. The Department approached me for help three years ago, knowing of my association with Barry Bourdain, and also of the friendships I have formed in New York's Chinatown. We have been after these men a long time, and Raintree and Bourdain have much to answer for."

"I know," Chance said. "I'm sorry, Cheng. Barry's not who we thought."

"Apparently none of us are." Kim's voice was dryly amused. "When this is over perhaps we can trade stories of our adventures."

"Later for that." The last piece had fallen into place. Now Chance was sure he knew who the killer was. His mind raced, discarding his original plans and creating new ones, calculating and reassessing, at such incredible speed that there was hardly even a noticeable pause before he added, "Cheng, I think I know how to smoke them all out. The show's still on for tonight?"

"There has been talk of canceling it. But I think everyone wants to go forward, as a sort of tribute to the fallen if nothing else." Kim paused. "What did you have in mind?"

"I think it's time for a return of the Flaming Coffin." Chance allowed himself a wicked smile. "Here's what we'll do...."

"The Flaming Coffin? Are you sure?" Martha Abbott blinked.

"Absolutely!" Glenn Saunders put enthusiasm into it. "I've spoken to my man Harper on the phone; he can bring us a suitable cabinet. I did it with Barry a hundred times. I think it would be a statement of... of proud defiance. We cannot be cowed by tragedy. The show must go on."

"Well...I don't know..." Martha sounded dubious.

"Let us have the theater for an hour or so," Glenn said. "We'll do a run-through and if it doesn't feel right, well of course we can cut it. But it was Barry's signature piece, Martha. Someone should do it."

A little more chivvying and Martha agreed, though it was clear she hated the idea. So it was that in another hour or so Joe Harper pulled up to the front entrance of the estate in a rental truck, and, with the help of Glenn and Cheng Kim, the latter looking extremely incongruous in a work shirt and blue jeans, but still sporting his lengthy pigtail, the three of them muscled the crate into the museum theater, where Merry and Tim were waiting.

As the three men wrestled the coffin-sized cabinet up on to the stage, Tiny Tim checked the theater's entrances and even glanced under the seats. "All clear."

Glenn nodded and Joe rapped sharply on the cabinet. Slowly the lid rose and George Chance emerged, dressed in the Ghost's green duster and ascot, but wearing his own face. "Well done, all of you. Hello, Cheng."

But Cheng was staring openmouthed at Chance, and then at Glenn Saunders, and then at Chance again. "Astonishing. Never in my life have I seen such a perfect double. And you are not related?"

"We're Siamese friends," Glenn replied, which gave Merry a case of the giggles.

Chance smiled as well, but grew serious quickly. "All right. Everyone knows about tonight? You spread the word?"

"Everyone," Merry assured him. "We talked it up all afternoon. Most folks think it's in poor taste but everyone is aware that the Flaming Coffin is on the schedule."

"Good. Cheng, where are your people?"

"I have arranged to meet them with Mr. Harper on the dirt road by the creek, where he heard the noises. An hour from now."

"One hopes you won't have long to wait." Chance paused. "Remember, all of you. Two people are already dead, and their only crime was being inconvenient. Our killer has been ahead of us all weekend, and is the most ruthless foe we've ever faced. I don't think I've ever seen anyone more careless of human life. Just…. Just be damn careful," he finished, lamely.

"That goes for you, too, kid," Tiny Tim put in, scowling. "This scheme of yours seems like a long shot at best. What if the murderer doesn't take the bait?"

Chance let out a short, bitter laugh. "You can trust me on that one. If you all have been talking up the Coffin I assure you our quarry will find it irresistible." He waved them away. "All right then. Scatter. And make sure you're seen," he added. "This only works if everyone thinks the theater is empty."

Everyone nodded and headed for the exits. Merry paused and gave Chance a brief hug. "You be careful, darlin'," she whispered. "Don't let him get in your head. Just take the son of a bitch down hard."

"Count on it." Chance smiled. "Now scat, I've got to get ready."

She let him go with reluctance and followed the others out. The theater went dark and Chance heard the click of a lock. He produced his jaw mask and makeup from one of the duster's voluminous pockets and set about transforming himself into the Green Ghost.

Then, spectral as his namesake, he moved silently to the rear of the theater, near the stage lighting control console, and settled in to wait.

An hour passed.

Then another.

Finally, after two hours and forty minutes, there was a creak from the stage. The Ghost tensed. He heard another creak, the rustle of clothing, and then a liquid slosh.

Showtime, he thought, and hit the lights.

A white spotlight suddenly illuminated the figure standing on the stage. He froze, paintbrush in hand, caught in the act of daubing some sort of clear liquid from a bucket on the stage floor on to the wooden cabinet.

It was the stooped, bearded figure of Jim Abbott. He glared up at the lights, his bristling beard and bushy eyebrows making him look somehow feral.

"That's accelerant in the bucket, isn't it?" The Ghost's voice rang out. "What is it? Gasoline? Magnesium nitrate? Is it what you used two years ago?"

The figure didn't move, but the expression in the eyes lost its anger, becoming instead something dark and sly. "Who's there?" he said slowly.

"Someone who's been waiting to bring you to account for a long time," the Ghost said. "Ever since that night in Edgarton two years ago."

"You *know*, don't you?" The man on the stage let out a rasping laugh. "I can tell. You're the Ghost. And you're one of mine. Have to be. I think it's Chance. Martha said it wasn't possible but I know it can't be anyone else. Not after the gymnastics last night. Come out where I can see you, Georgie."

"All right." The Green Ghost stepped forward a little. "Now it's your turn. Lose the beard and the wig. It makes me sick to look at you standing there like that, disguised as the man you murdered."

"Fair enough," said the man on the stage. He tore off the white wig and beard, and stood up straight. "How's that?"

"Still unbelievable." The Ghost shook his head. "I can't imagine what happened to turn you into what you are. But even seeing your face… it's almost impossible to believe that I'm looking at Barry Bourdain."

"That's because you're a sucker, Georgie. It is Georgie under all that Lon Chaney makeup, isn't it?" Bourdain squinted. "Hard to tell with that light in my eyes. Let me…"

"Don't move an inch," the Ghost snapped. "I've got you covered." He moved forward a little more so Bourdain could see the pistol in his hand.

"Guns? Really?" Bourdain just looked amused. "I remember you as more of a knife-throwing guy, Georgie. That circus upbringing."

"The knife's in another pocket. For this a gun seemed advisable."

"Ah. Makes sense." Bourdain stretched, luxuriously, like a cat. "Nice not to have to stoop," he added. "When did you know? What gave me away?"

"No one thing. Lots of little ones. The showmanship. The misdirection. The layers of needless complexity to hide something very simple. Magician's trademarks. *Your* trademarks." The Ghost's voice held anger now. "And really it was something as old as humanity, something someone said to me before we ever came up here. Money and a woman. You were having an affair with Martha. And you were financing your showbiz lifestyle with the smuggling. There never was anyone named Raintree, never any hidden money, was there? It was you. *You* were Raintree."

Bourdain just chuckled. "You were always so smart. Smartest one I ever had," he added. "Tell me more."

"You're stalling."

"What's your hurry?"

"All right." The Ghost shrugged. "It was the real Jim Abbott on stage that night in Edgarton, right? That was your plan. His burned body would be mistaken for yours, an accidental death so spectacular and awful no one would question it. There would be no investigation, no snoopy coroner checking dental records or anything like that. And then you could just step in and assume his identity. How did you get him up here from Manhattan that night?"

"He came on his own," Bourdain said. "He was in New York on business, investigating my finances. He'd figured it out about the Raintree identity. And because we were friends, instead of going straight to the feds he came to me first, drove up that night to meet me in my dressing room in the theater. Just showed up and started yelling at me. He left me no choice," he added. "And then I saw a perfect way out, a way for Barry Bourdain to disappear and yet not go anywhere at all. So I hit him and straitjacketed him and stuffed him in a bag, soaked it in the kerosene mix I used for the flash cloth, and I told Martha what I had in mind. Of course, she thought Jim's death was an accident. I told her that he'd attacked me in a jealous rage and he'd hit his head while I was defending myself. But I persuaded her that faking my death would free us to be together, and she was willing to help on that basis. She really loves me, you know."

"I can see why. Such a catch you are." The Green Ghost snorted. "Racketeering. Murder."

"Oh, step off your high horse, Georgie." Bourdain looked annoyed now. "I saw an advantage and I used it. Abbott would have destroyed me. I just got to him first."

"So you disappeared after the stage fire, stopped on your way out to torch the Raintree warehouse, and were in Manhattan by morning to take over as Jim Abbott. And no one noticed, no one ever realized that they were talking to a completely different man." The Ghost's voice sharpened. "Even if Jim's death was a twisted kind of self-defense, which I don't buy for a second, what was Anthony? He was nobody."

"He saw me," Bourdain snapped. "Out on the grounds at night, on my way to meet Raintree's suppliers. Twice. The second time, last night, he took me by surprise and he was going to start shouting. Came tearing out on to the lawn saying he'd seen me from the upstairs window. So I had to. Anyway he wouldn't shut up about seeing the ghost of Barry Bourdain. Sooner or later someone smart, like you, Georgie, would have figured it out. Hell, you *did* figure it out."

"Only because of that convoluted story Martha told," The Ghost was not bothering to hide his anger now, almost spitting the words. "It wasn't anything Anthony said or did. It was Martha. At first, last night, she thought I knew it all and blamed her equally for Jim's murder. I almost had her broken, until I made the mistake of mentioning 'her husband.' Then her whole demeanor changed. She realized I'd missed the most important part; that it was all *you,* all along. She spun out a ridiculous story about an out-of-work actor and Raintree being on your trail and how you'd planned this whole weekend to try and catch him. Stalling until you came upstairs and heard us talking, and could come in with the rifle." He paused. "Speaking of this weekend, that's the part that baffles me. Why the hell even host it? Why a Bourdain museum?"

"Because, you damn fool," Bourdain said, "I wasn't going to go around as a hunchback with a phony beard forever. I was going to stage a comeback. Reclaim my own identity. But first I had to make sure that none of you boys would ever put it together, you were the only ones that knew the Flaming Coffin well enough to realize what really happened that night. A weekend up here with kindly Jim and Martha would let me look all of you over. The show was just in case I needed to stage an accident. There never were any permissions, no advertising. We were going to be all alone up here. Then I figured with Anthony dead, everyone would want to cancel. But not George Chance, oh, no. He wants to do a tribute to his poor dead friend." He shook his head bitterly. "I can't believe I fell for it. Reeled me in like a bass."

"I knew you would want George Chance disposed of, after you caught him looking at the straitjacket," the Ghost said. "You put it on display deliberately, to see who would react to it. And then when Anthony became too nosy, you decided they both had to go. Kill Anthony outright and stage an accident here for Chance. With Chance dead too, you could blame everything on him; Anthony's murder, the Green Ghost, all of it. So we set you up. I knew the great Barrett Bourdain couldn't resist having the Flaming Coffin end in drama and tragedy once again. It was just a matter of waiting for you to show up here to sabotage the act. Showmanship and misdirection, Barry. You taught us all well."

"Not as well as you think, Georgie." Bourdain had been inching closer to the bucket of accelerant and suddenly he swung down and scooped it up, hurling it at the Ghost. Instantly the skull-faced figure was covered with sharp-smelling gasoline. "You don't dare fire that pistol now." Bourdain produced a box of wooden matches and lit one, holding the tiny flame out in front of him like a talisman. "Now, I'm going back out through the stage door and you're going to stand very still. Or poof." He started to back slowly away from the Ghost, but stopped. "You know, I think it may be poof anyway..."

Before Bourdain could throw the burning match, the Ghost leaped to the side, and whipped out his thin throwing knife. He flipped it forward, underhand, in one smooth motion. It caught Bourdain in the wrist of his upraised hand, embedding itself neatly between the tendons there. Bourdain screamed...

--and dropped the lit match.

The puddle of accelerant on the floor in front of Bourdain went up in a sheet of flame, as did the coffin-shaped box behind him that he had been painting with the stuff. In a second Bourdain was inside a small inferno. Still screaming, holding his wrist with the knife sticking out of it, Bourdain tried to jump clear but his foot caught on a corner of the box and he fell face-first into the fire. His clothing had picked up enough of the stuff that instantly he was aflame as well. His screams turned into a gurgle, and then silence.

The fire continued to burn. The Green Ghost knew he had to put it out and alert the household, but horror held him for a moment and he just stood and stared at his former mentor's burning body.

The theater entrance doors burst open. It was Glenn and Merry.

"What the hell, boss?" Glenn burst out.

"It's Barry Bourdain," the Green Ghost said, heavily. "In his flaming coffin." He took a deep breath and exhaled, shuddering. "I guess I really am more of a knife guy."

Two weeks later, at Chance's 54th Street brownstone, a rare occasion was taking place; George Chance and Glenn Saunders were at the same dinner table, along with several other guests. Merry, Tiny Tim, Joe Harper, and, no longer pigtailed, Cheng Kim, looking very Westernized in a white linen suit with a blue shirt and darker blue tie.

"You wouldn't have believed what we found out there," Harper was saying. "It went just like you thought it would, boss; we found Martha

Abbott coming out a tunnel entrance practically on top of that bend in the creek where I was that night. She was packing up to make a run for it. When Cheng and the feds bagged her she gave it all up." Harper paused for effect, then delivered his bombshell. "You know that whining I thought I heard that night? It was real. There was ten Chinese girls chained up in the room she showed us. Plus crates of dope, and even guns and grenades. Bourdain was no piker."

"He certainly wasn't," Cheng Kim said quietly. "According to Martha Abbott, once Bourdain orchestrated his return from the dead he was also going to relaunch the Raintree smuggling operation, bigger than ever before. Martha Abbott's testimony helped us to round up the men involved with that as well, including the one that threatened Mr. Harper."

"So that's a wrap, then," Tim said. "Hard to believe that about Martha. I can't figure how she could get herself in so deep with Bourdain."

"She loved him," Kim said. "He was a monster. But she loved him all the same."

"So awful." Merry shuddered, then abruptly turned and elbowed George Chance. "You're awfully quiet. What's bringing you down? It's a party."

Chance smiled, but only half-heartedly. "I was just thinking about Barry. And his legacy. I got into this because I wanted his name to mean something. And now it does… it means murder and horror and everything we saw up in Edgarton. Selling young girls, for God's sake."

"Oh, for…" Merry swatted Chance on the arm. "All right, gloomy Gus, but you can think about this, too. Bourdain's legacy includes *you*. And Cheng here, about to go be the head T-man for upstate New York. You men have done remarkable things, you've saved lives, you've done *good*. That ought to wash the Bourdain stain off. He did what he did. So what? How does that reflect on you or Cheng or any of you? His crimes have nothing to do with the skills you learned from him or who you are."

"I suppose." Chance shook his head. "I just… I was so wrong about him. And Martha."

"Does you good to be wrong once in a while." Merry flashed a smile. "And us too. It gets tiring being surrounded by so much damn genius all the time." She turned to face Glenn Saunders and glared combatively at him. "And you? What's your gripe? You've been as quiet as George tonight."

"Oh, it's not a big deal," Glenn said. "I feel kind of petty even mentioning it. That Saturday up in Edgarton doubling the boss, getting hammered by Inspector Ludgate, all of that, was the hardest thing I've ever done, and I sure hope I don't have to do that again anytime soon. But…" He paused, and then plunged ahead. "I *was* kind of looking forward to doing a real show in front of an audience."

"That's show business, kid," Tiny Tim said, and lit a cigar.

THE END

THOUGHTS ON THE GREEN GHOST

"First principles," is what I always tell my students in Young Authors. "The hero of the story *defines* the story. The lead shouldn't be just some plot-moving robot; the plot is moved forward by who your hero actually *is.*"

I wasn't all that familiar with the Green Ghost when I took this on, other than knowing he was one more of those wealthy young crimefighters in a mask who were *Like The Shadow, But Not.* So, following my own advice, I had to figure out who George Chance was and what set him apart from the other costumed pulp heroes of the thirties and forties. I had read one of the Ghost's exploits in John Gunnison's wonderful reprint series *High Adventure*—which you all should be reading too, if you like pulp fiction— and I pulled that out and looked at it again, and also invested in another Green Ghost reprint paperback collection from *Pulp Tales Presents.* After reading the original Green Ghost adventures, several things jumped out at me.

The stories were actual mysteries with a classic structure; the Ghost has a lot more in common with Ellery Queen or Philo Vance than he does with his other costumed contemporaries. And George Chance, as a character, never seemed too terribly challenged by his adventures. He was always ahead of things, always a little condescending. But most of all, the thing that set him apart was that he was a showbiz guy, raised in the circus, who grew up to be a famous stage magician. All his aides are circus or stage types: a dwarf, a showgirl, a carnival barker, and a stunt double. I figured I would build my story around those ideas.

Michael Panush already had zeroed in on the circus background as the hook for his story, so I started thinking about stage magic. A classic whodunit murder mystery, built on the themes of illusion and misdirection, where everyone has a secret, and most are using a stage persona to hide the real person beneath. I wanted George Chance to face a real challenge, as well, something he'd really have to work at to pull out the win. So I gave him a houseful of suspects who knew all his tricks, who would be the least likely to be frightened or fooled by the Green Ghost's usual repertoire, and who would be just as deft and clever at misdirection and illusion as he was himself. I also wanted Chance to be really personally invested for once, and to be wrong and make mistakes he'd have to recover from. I think a hero who has to bounce back from a defeat is way more interesting than one who's never wrong or in any real danger... and I liked the idea that in order to crack the case, Chance has to let go of some of his own most cherished illusions.

My original notion was to set the action at a casino in Atlantic City, but Ron Fortier suggested it would work better at a private mansion somewhere in upstate New York, and I want to be sure he gets credit for that because that lent a great Gothic atmosphere to the whole thing and instantly unlocked several plot issues I was having. I even found a photo of a Victorian-era "masonry Gothic" mansion in Tarrytown that was so ideal for what I had in mind for the Bourdain Museum that I instantly appropriated it for this story.

I did other research too. My wife teases me about how I'll be lucky to break even on these pulp stories I write because I always end up buying a bunch of books to look things up, but part of the fun of writing these is the research. Because I'm a big nerd, that's why. In particular, I needed to know more about stage magic, its traditions and history. Far and away, the most helpful books I found were *Secrets of Magic – Ancient and Modern* and *The Master Magicians,* both authored by the king of the pulps: Walter Gibson, the man behind the Shadow. I read up on Houdini and Blackstone and Thurston and, my favorite just for his sheer oddity, Billy Robinson, who assumed the identity of the Chinese "Chung Ling Soo" not just on stage but also in his real life. Robinson lived as Soo for years, complete with pigtail, and refused even to speak with reporters unless he had a Chinese interpreter. He was too perfect a character for a story about illusion and false identity for me not to make use of him, and so my own "Cheng Kim" is based on Mr. Robinson; however, I felt the implied racism was so blatant in the history of the real Chung Ling Soo that I made my fake Chinaman a supercool Treasury agent working undercover to try and compensate for it. (Sadly, the real Chung Ling Soo died on stage in a botched bullet-catching trick, in 1918.)

I also watched DVDs a friend burned for me of a wonderful, largely-forgotten 1970s TV show called *The Magician,* starring Bill Bixby. Bixby played a wealthy stage magician who solved crimes with the aid of his private jet's pilot and an eccentric news columnist. More than anything else, it was Bixby's *Magician* that I was thinking of when I was writing about the kind of guy George Chance was, and "Blake Anthony" is my little nod to Bixby's Anthony Blake.

So that's where it all came from. All that's left are the thank-yous; to Ron for his helpful editorial suggestions, to my beta reading crew Anne Hawley, Edward Bosnar, Sena Meilleur, Lorinda Adams, and Brekke Ferguson, all of whom prevented me from embarrassing myself with silly mistakes any number of times... and of course to my wife Julie, who puts up with all this obsessive writerly madness and even claims to find it endearing.

And thank *you*, readers, for checking our stuff out. I hope enough of you out there enjoyed this volume that we get to do more Green Ghost books for you. I have to confess that I didn't think much of George Chance when I first encountered him in print, but I got rather attached to the Ghost and his posse while I was working on this. It's the most fun I've had on any 'new pulp' project so far, and I'd love to visit the Green Ghost's world again.

GREG HATCHER - has been writing for one outlet or another for the last twenty-plus years, but his stories for Airship 27 are his first published-for-real pulp fiction and he's still grinning about it. You can find his weekly column on the website ComicBookResources.com, as one of the regular rotating features on Comics Should Be Good. In addition to writing, he also teaches both the Cartooning and Young Authors classes for grades seven through twelve as part of an afterschool arts program in Seattle. He lives in Burien, Washington with his wife Julie, their cat Maggie, and ten thousand books and comics.

THE CASE OF THE ROCKETEER RIPPER

B. C. Bell

"If my mom only knew I was driving around teaching sailors how to cheat at cards," the tiny brunette in the passenger seat said. She held the back of her hand to her head in a melodramatic martyr's salute. "An innocent girl like me swept away by the magic fingers of a circus boy."

George Chance laughed as he pulled the large sedan out of a gas station and onto the highway. Since he'd retired from the most successful career of any magician known, he had not been idle. For the last three months, Chance had been touring military bases, along with his favorite assistant, Merry White, demonstrating to American servicemen the most common tricks and cons used by some of the dodgier gambling establishments that tended to surround military towns.

"Games of chance are as old as humanity, Merry. I just figured I'd do my part in wartime and help our boys hang on to a bit of their hard earned cash," the magician criminologist said. "And we both know wherever soldiers and sailors gather there's going to be gambling."

"I thought wherever soldiers and sailors gathered there was a fight," Merry White said. She was a petite young lady, Miss Merry White, with shiny green eyes and black hair, but the booking agents who measured her personality in megawatts didn't have the advantage that George Chance had. She was the woman of interest in his life. The girl who knew all his secrets.

"Well, if I can steer them away from the con games and the boys have more money in their wallet, maybe there'll be a few less fights." Chance pointed at a highway sign proclaiming their destination to be only twenty miles away. "Besides, this trip's not all business. I'm meeting up with an old friend before the seminar, Judd Walters."

"The kid that used to build the rigged games for the circus midway?" Merry feigned a wide, green eyed shock.

"The very same. He worked for the circus during the summers while he went to college. He does design research for the government now."

"Well, I guess that's a step up from rigging the ring toss," Merry said. "What sort of stuff is he designing?"

"I don't know, supposed to be 'Top Secret.' He majored in engineering in school, was one of Robert Goddard's students."

"Rocketry," Merry said. "Well, if the government doesn't work out, he can always go back to the circus and run the fireworks show."

"From the letters he's written, it sounds like the only fireworks show he'll be putting on will be for our Axis enemies. He does some sort of aircraft, fighter design, but it's all very hush-hush. Unfortunately, he's been disappointed in the progress whatever he's working on is making. I'm afraid his last letter seemed very frustrated. I thought we'd pop in and cheer him up while we're here. He lives just off the lake by Fort Burlington. We might even be able to get in some fishing."

"I think I'd rather go where the soldiers and sailors are fighting," Merry said.

They checked themselves into Burlington's finest hotel, which wasn't much by Manhattan standards, but did have two adjoining suites on the top floor.

Burlington was an entire town built around and tailored to the Army base of the same name. As such, the major places of business were like those found in a small town square, the hotel, a bar, a bank, a grocery store, and a gas station. Behind those staples of modern American life, on the side of town furthest from the actual fort, sat sketchier bars, the gambling joints, strip clubs, and a dance hall full of young dime a dance girls.

Headed for their friend, Judd Walter's house, George and Merry went in the other direction. Chance pointed toward the Aerodyne Industries laboratories where the scientist worked, separated from the fort by only a wall and a half mile of lawn with a looping drive in front of it. Driving past the scenic lake, the scenery became more that of a small forest instead of an army base. Still, all one had to do was drive down a tarmac road to the laboratories.

Winding down the trail to Judd Walters' cabin, the curve of the path suddenly revealed two Burlington Police cars, their emergency lights cutting through the late afternoon dimness of the forest. Chance parked the car and jumped out of the vehicle. A uniformed policeman stopped him in the yard.

"What happened?" George Chance said.

"Are you a friend of Dr. Walters, Mr. Chance?" the policeman asked, recognizing the world famous magician.

"Yes, an old friend. We used to work together."

The policeman's eyes seemed to widen a little, surprised to see a celebrity on the scene. "Well, Mr. Chance, sir, I hate to be the one to tell you this, but I'm afraid he's... no longer with us."

"You mean," Chance hesitated, "he's dead?"

"Cleaning lady found the body this afternoon, sir."

"Foul play?" George Chance asked.

"The foulest I've ever seen."

George Chance asked to meet the man in charge, and Chief Buford Deighton came to the door. Like most of the general public, the Chief was vaguely familiar with Chance's work in the field of criminology and invited him in. Chance and the Chief shuffled inside, making sure to stay out of the way of the crime scene investigator going through the drawers and dusting for prints.

Once in the cabin, the Chief admitted, "So far there's not much to go on."

There on the floor lay the body of Dr. Judd Walters, headless. The head sat severed above the neck like it had just popped off. The body wore a freshly laundered lab coat.

"Where's the blood?" was the first thing Chance said. There was little blood on the rug or floorboards around it.

"No signs of a struggle, either," Chief Deighton said. "Nothing appears to be missing..."

"Other than the neck between his shoulders and his head," Merry said. She'd somehow managed to sneak around the officer at the door.

"Whoa! This is a crime scene!" Chief Deighton jumped toward the door, trying to cover Merry's eyes with the palm of his hand. "There's no need for you to have to see this, ma'am."

Merry's hand still covered her mouth, but after her initial gasp, she'd recovered quicker than any of the local police. This wasn't her first murder scene.

"Too late, Chief." She angled her head over Deighton's shoulder. "But I have to say of all the bodies I've seen sawn in half, that one's the most realistic."

"Permit me to introduce my assistant and friend, Miss Merry White," Chance said.

"Oh...then...well, pleasure to meet you Miss White." The Chief lowered the bill of his cap and, once again, examined the body of Dr. Walters. "I just wish we could've met under better circumstances."

"Poor Judd," Merry said, staring in sad but unabashed fascination at the body. "I was hoping to congratulate him. He'd come so far."

George Chance, who'd been surveying the room while the other two spoke, kneeled down next to the body and began to inspect the wound. He pulled a pencil out of his pocket and pointed to the slice that severed the neck.

"This is one of the cleanest cuts I've ever seen," Chance said. "Like a razor. May I?" He pointed at one of the body's pockets with the pencil.

Chief Deighton nodded.

Emptying the pockets Chance found no keys, only Dr. Walters' wallet, a pack of cigarettes, and some rationing cards.

"So whoever hid the body, probably took the keys." Chance laid out the evidence on the floor in front of the Sheriff, taking extra precaution to shove the wallet and rationing tickets into his view. "Doesn't look like a robbery, either."

"Not unless we they were going to steal his head and the maid walked in on the act," Merry said.

The Chief started to answer, but then heard Chance almost chuckle under his breath. Merry had a way of defusing these intense situations.

"No, whatever happened didn't happen here," Chance said, "which means we're starting at a disadvantage. The success or failure of many a homicide investigation involves processing the scene of the crime and in this case, we don't have one. Do you know if Dr. Walters had any enemies?"

"Hard to tell, but doubtful. He spent most of his time at the Aerodyne laboratories. Went to church on Sunday. Went grocery shopping and fishing once a week. Seemed friendly enough." He waved a hand over the body. "Just between you and me, I don't see any solid suspects."

"Any ideas on what might have motivated such a thing?"

"None yet, like I said, he kept to himself mostly. I've already called the judge for search warrants at both his Fort Burlington office and Aerodyne labs, but unfortunately, we won't be able to get anything done until tomorrow. Aerodyne Industries may not be listed as part of the federal government but they might as well be. Everything they do over there is hush-hush, and you have to wrangle your way between the locals, the state and the feds. This could get complicated."

"Mind if I ask a few questions while I'm in town, Chief?"

"Feel free, Mr. Chance," Chief Deighton said. "Given your reputation it would be a pleasure. In fact, when those warrants and the lab results come in I'd be glad to give you a call. I need as many qualified hands on a case like this as I can get."

The two men exchanged phone numbers and handshakes.

"It was a pleasure meeting y'all," Chief Deighton said. "I'll give you a ring as soon as I know anything."

On their way to the car outside, Merry leaned toward George Chance, magician-criminologist extraordinaire, and whispered.

"I saw that gleam in your eye, darlin'." She climbed in the car and closed the doors shut. "And, I have a feeling a certain green friend of ours is not going to be nearly as patient as Chief Deighton."

"No, I'm afraid the Green Ghost can't afford to wait. If Chief Deighton called in the FBI, their investigators may mark everything 'Top Secret' and shut this case down immediately. I'm going to need you to reserve two rooms at that tiny hotel we saw on the edge of town, and give our friends Joe Harper and Glenn Saunders a call.

"He may have just been a carnival barker when I knew him, but Dr. Judd Walters was still a friend. So, the Green Ghost should be paying a visit to Aerodyne Industries tonight."

Aerodyne Industries sat next to Fort Burlington, separated by only a circular driveway and large front yard. The building stood in a squat and long rectangle, almost tube-shaped on top, with a white dome in the middle. The impression given by the building's traditional gothic look outside masked the fact that some of the highest tech experiments in flight design and rocket guidance known to man went on inside.

Two guards in towers stood on patrol at the back corners of Fort Burlington, the lighted yards surrounding Aerodyne Industries easily visible. Another night watchman stood at attention in front of the Aerodyne building, while another patrolled the yard, circling the building every twenty minutes.

Scanning the yard from the forest scrub on the other side of the road as work shifts changed, the Green Ghost estimated two more watchmen to be at work inside the building. He had also spotted electrical contacts on the building's doors and windows, most likely connected to an alarm system. There might even be a vacuum tube–powered motion sensitive alarm sensors inside.

George Chance smiled to himself in the shadows. Nothing was top secret to a Ghost.

Growing up in the circus, Chance had learned more than just the rudiments of magic. Impersonation, trapeze, gymnastics, knife-throwing, and a great deal of showmanship, but, from Ricky the Clown he had learned the art of make-up, and soon surpassed his teacher.

Kneeling behind the shelter of a murky oak, George Chance opened a small leather pouch and began to apply his skillful fingers to his face. He inserted wire ovals into his nostrils, much like Lon Chaney had in *The Phantom of the Opera*, broadening his nose and tilting his lips. Brown pigment deepened the effect, making it look like he had two open sinus cavities in his head. Added to the hollows of his cheeks and eyes, the pigment gave one the appearance of the walking dead. He covered his own pearly white teeth with a set of dull, yellowed, celluloid choppers, then applied a bit more of a ghostly pallor by hitting his cheeks with some powder.

Already dressed in his special, reversible green suit, Chance had numerous tricks hidden in an array of secret pockets; tricks that had proven themselves timeless against an army of underworld evildoers. He had a knife up one sleeve, and a gun rig that would pop a .45 automatic into his hand with a flick of his wrist up the other. A black crusher hat soon shrouded his eyes, and the Green Ghost was back.

Luckily for the Ghost, the property surrounding Aerodyne Industries that wasn't Fort Burlington was mostly forest and scrub, live and dead trees interspersed with thick undergrowth. The murky features of the Ghost seemed to blend with the early morning fog and vine-covered timbers of the forest's rotting timbers, as if he'd been given birth by them.

Reaching into one of his many trick pockets the Green Ghost removed two small spring-loaded spools of nylon, similar to fishing line. He tied the end of one line to a large hedge amidst a patch of reeds and began to twist his way silently through the briar and moss, not once disturbing the delicate underbrush or shaking the bush to which the line was attached. He made his way to the northwest corner of the property and attached the spool to the limbs of a tree about twenty feet from the property line.

He then crept back to the northern border, the property directly in back of the Aerodyne building, with the second spool and repeated the procedure, once again, tying the line of the second spool to the same tree limb.

The special spools were designed to yank things out of the viewer's way when a magician made something "disappear." They could be used to pull something up your sleeve, up in the air, or, if planned right ahead of time, even behind the viewer, so that with a wave of a hand, almost anything could vanish.

Of course, the Green Ghost wasn't using these wind-up spools to make something disappear. He was going to use them to make something appear where it wasn't.

On the South side of the property, opposite the lines he'd set up on the northwest side, the Green Ghost sat perched in the crook of a tree, waiting, as the watchman on patrol marched by almost facing him, but never able to see him. That was the genius of the Ghost's disguise. With the muted shades of his suit and crusher hat he could blend with almost any surrounding.

In Chance's own words, the Ghost was two faced. In the shadows he was hard to see. In a crowd he appeared to be just another anonymous, obscure figure with a shade of night club pallor. Not until George Chance "turned on" the Green Ghost would he be noticed.

This change initiated itself through Chance's physical mastery of his facial muscles and was so extreme as to even affect his demeanor. With but a laugh, his lips would pull back to reveal the ivory jawed death's head of the emerald specter. A vacant stare, intensified by the make-up, made his eyes appear empty. And if he needed a little extra intimidation, the Ghost could illuminate his skull face with a hidden, green light mounted on a scarf pin he wore. Those who had witnessed the grisly visage of the Ghost encased in the green light never forgot it.

The Green Ghost looked up from his watch the exact same time the bushes on the opposite side of the property began to shake. He'd purposely made sure the bushes were within the view of the front door guard.

"I've got a visual disturbance in the north field!"

From his vantage point the Ghost could see the front door watchman yell for assistance. The watchman patrolling around the building was currently behind it. He stood, suddenly at alert, then hollered back and began running toward the front of the building.

The Green Ghost watched as the two men met at the building's entrance, each leaning forward as they spoke. Unfortunately, there was no way for the Ghost to follow the conversation. One of the guards turned and began marching toward the tiny hedge of reeds jumping in the night, his pistol drawn.

Directly to the guard's left, along the western line of the property, bushes began to shake and vibrate. The guard motioned with his gun, indicating he would investigate the bushes on the west side, and the other guard should investigate the jumping reeds along the north side of the building.

The Ghost, still seated in his tree on the opposite side, eyed the guards in the towers at the rear of Fort Burlington. They had their eyes on the bushes, too.

No normal man could have ever crossed that brightly lit yard unseen, but the Ghost did. Swinging from the highest branch he could reach, he launched himself onto the south end of the property. He hit the ground, almost running, but fell into a roll. With nothing to hide behind, the roll served only to slow him enough that he wouldn't be detected. Then, with three powerful strides, the Ghost was hidden behind the five-foot brick wall that surrounded Aerodyne Industries garbage drop off. At the edge of the enclosure they had been kind enough to install a window in the building.

With one glance, the Ghost recognized the electrical contacts that ran a connection between the window sash and its frame, part of the alarm system.

Reaching into one of his many pockets, Chance removed an insulated piece of copper wire with a clip on each end. Using a pair of portable wire clippers, he bared the wire on both side of the electrical contacts attached to the window. He then clipped his own copper wire to the bared wires, thus creating a false electrical connection. Now when he opened the window, the electrical security system would "read" that the window's electrical contacts had never been broken.

Listening as one of the guards cursed "the damn kids and their gags" in front of the building, the Ghost shoved the window sash wide. Placing both hands on top of the brick wall, the Ghost hoisted himself in the air and swung inside like a gymnast, legs first.

Landing on the floor, he melted back into the walls. He was in an office with desks to hide behind if he should need them. He wouldn't.

He pulled the insulated wire clippers out of his pocket again, and pulled a short piece of insulated wire from his pocket. Baring both ends of the wire, he bent it into a U-shape, then, still holding the wire in the center with the insulated pliers, shoved both ends of it into an electrical socket. Sparks popped, and a distant hum seemed to stop. Though few lights were on, he could feel the drone of the building's power cease to exist. He'd knocked out the electricity.

That would send the two night watchmen on duty inside the building down to the basement to look at the fuse box. Now he had to find Dr. Judd Walter's office.

The Ghost seemed to float down the hall, his head pivoting as he glanced inside offices and the names on their doors. Still searching for the lab, he climbed a short set of stairs to a door marked "Do Not Enter."

Inside, it looked almost like a warehouse. A long tube surrounded by glass with a large fan on one side of its length indicated he was in some sort of wind tunnel.

He'd knocked out the electricity.

Of course, Chance thought, *Judd was researching flight design. The use of a wind tunnel would be paramount in the design of missiles and aircraft.*

Shading a penlight with the fingers of his hand, the Ghost decided to risk putting a little light on the situation. On the other end of the tunnel was a glass enclosed office, most likely used by the observers of wind experiments. In other words, a lab.

Looking out from the laboratory he could see mounts on the walls where engines and wings had been tested. Going through the drawers he found no notes. He had to find Dr. Walters' office. For the briefest of seconds he shined his flashlight into the corners and across the ceiling of the wind tunnel. One of the reinforced glass panels on the top right hand side of the tunnel was broken open, half the glass cracked off.

Odd for a state-of-the-art research facility, the Ghost thought. He left the lab through its back door, circled around to the outside of the wind tunnel and retrieved a shard of glass about two inches square. He stuck the glass into an envelope and into one of his many pockets so he could look at it under a microscope later.

Dr. Walters' office sat on the second floor. The place was a mess, as if someone had been rifling through his papers. Maybe after his unfortunate death, the rest of the employees wanted to see where his work was going, but the murder, having just occurred, most likely hadn't been reported to them until after closing time. There was no way of telling.

The Ghost sighed and began to rifle through the desk, all the time listening for the night watchmen who might reappear at any given moment. The notes on the desk were technical, no sketches or blueprints, just mathematical formulas. It would take a rocket scientist to figure them out. After thumbing through the file cabinet he began searching behind pictures on the wall and beneath drawers. Taped to the bottom of the middle right-hand desk drawer the Ghost found what he was looking for, a notebook with leather binding.

Stuffed between the pages of the notebook, pictures and copies of business forms stuck out at all angles. The Ghost had to put the notes on the desk to keep them from falling all over the floor, but the handwriting inside looked the same as the handwriting on the desk paperwork, it was Dr. Judd Walters.

Not wanting to interfere with the federal investigation to come, the Ghost couldn't just pocket the diary and run. Instead, the Ghost whipped a miniature camera, smaller than a pack of cigarettes, out of the pockets his suit.

The camera clicked on every page. Then the Ghost taped Dr. Walter's journal back to the bottom of the drawer where he'd found it.

Skulking back down the hall, the Ghost felt the power humming through the building again. Several desk lamps and sconces in the hall lit up. The Ghost took the rear stairs three at a time. Stopping on the ground floor, he could hear the voices of the night watchmen inside returning to their regular duties.

"You check the back again. I'll check the front," One of them said.

The guard closest walked directly toward the door the Ghost hid behind. The nearest office was a hundred feet away. The guard sprung the door open, and then turned to face his partner.

"While you're up there, you might want to ask those guys outside what all the ruckus was about? Something weird going on here tonight." Then turning back around, he walked down the hall.

If he had bothered to look up, the night watchman would have seen the Green Ghost above him, next to the ceiling his feet mounted on one wall, his hands on another, holding him suspended in the air. But the guard didn't look up. The Ghost was grateful for that, and for the fact that these men hadn't been issued the new walkie-talkies, hand held radios, that the Army kept talking about. While he wished the best for America's troops, the Ghost knew that had these men been better equipped he'd be in jail.

Sheltering himself in the shadows of the corner maintenance room, the Ghost waited for the guards to return to their regular rounds. A half hour later, he was back in the basement, raiding one of the watchmen's lockers where he found an extra uniform. Slipping back upstairs to a corner office, he set a pile of paper on fire in the wastebasket and made his way back to the window he'd broken in earlier.

With the power back on, the night watchmen wasted no time calling for help. Ten minutes later the place was flooded with police, firemen, and a few uniformed Army officers. In all the excitement, no one noticed the guard with the death's head face making his way to the southwest corner of the property to disappear in the thick woods.

Chance removed his disguise, and then drove back to the hotel with the pictures he'd taken of Dr. Walters' journal.

The next morning the summer sun was warm and bright, the trees blooming in stark contrast to the murder that dwelt in the city of Burlington. While driving to the hotel on the edge of town to meet with the Green Ghost's aides, George and Merry ran into a roadblock. Several bulldozers and a steamroller filled the right hand lane of the road. In passing, Chance noticed some tax-exempt government plates on one of the cars parked by the construction site and pulled over. Two men held a conversation on the edge of the site, one of them pointing from one direction to the other. One wore khakis and a denim shirt, the other a suit. Chance guessed one of them was the construction foreman and the other an employee of the city of Burlington.

"Morning, gentleman." Chance stepped out of the car. "I didn't notice any construction going on here yesterday. Everything all right?"

The man in the suit smiled, and ran a hand across his black comb-over, while the man in khakis ran a hand through his red hair looking agitated. It was easy for Chance to tell the man in the khakis was the job foreman.

"Everything's fine, sir," the man in the suit said, with a practiced, almost Southern accent. "Standard maintenance, as promised to the good people of Burlington and anybody travelling through it." He held out his hand. "Mayor Edmund MacAfee."

"George Chance," the world famous illusionist said, shaking his hand unassumingly.

"George Chance? The magician? Well, I'll be! I thought I recognized you," Mayor MacAfee said. "My wife and I saw you make an elephant disappear in New York a few years back! Never could figure out how you pulled that off."

"Pleasure to meet you, Mr. Chance," the man in khaki's said. "I'm Stannard Reinhardt."

Chance almost flinched in surprise. "'The' Stannard Reinhardt? Owner of Aerodyne Industries?"

"Among other things," Reinhardt answered and pointed at the road. "Anything I can do to help out the community that helps Aerodyne."

Having just broken into the man's property the night before, Chance almost felt like hiding his face but shook his hand instead.

"You got somebody guarding all this oil?" Merry White yelled, standing next to a tractor and pointing to five rows of metal drums stacked by the road. While the men had been talking, Merry had snuck out of the car and started to explore. "This stuff would be worth a fortune to wartime black marketers!"

Reinhardt turned with a jerk, apparently upset by the woman on his construction site.

"And, that, sirs, is my lovely assistant, Miss Merry White." Chance waved a hand as if presenting her on stage, and the three men wandered down the road where Merry was. "You'll have to forgive her curiosity. It's probably what led her to become a magician's assistant to begin with."

The men chuckled in a businesslike fashion. It had more to do with being polite than being funny.

"No, seriously," Merry said, "There's enough oil here to fill a thousand ration books. All it would take was a farmer with a truck and he could open his own gas station."

"I wouldn't worry too much, Miss White," Reinhardt said. "That's not oil in those barrels. It's a special sealant we're using to fill the porous spaces in the tar and cement. But, thanks for pointing that out. Even though I have a night watchman on the site, I really should have those barrels labeled."

"I understand you're going to be putting on a show for our boys at Camp Burlington tonight, Mr. Chance," the Mayor said.

"Oh, not so much a show as a seminar. I'm going to teach them some of the dishonest tricks of the gambling trade so at least if they're gambling, they won't be losing it all to a crooked house."

"Will you be performing any tricks?" The mayor's feet shifted beneath him like a child asking for ice cream.

"Well, it's really meant to be more of an informal seminar, Mr. Mayor. But, yes, magic tricks have been known to occur."

The mayor's feet danced, like a child who had asked for ice cream and his parent's had said yes. "I hope you don't mind, Mr. Chance, but since Fort Burlington is the heart of this city, I asked the General if a few of the city fathers might attend."

"The more the merrier, Mayor McAfee. While some of the dodgier roadhouses around here might take offense, I don't see any problems with a well-informed public. Will you be attending, Mr. Reinhardt?"

"Well, we have some federal men coming into town to investigate the death of one of my employees, so I'll most likely be going wherever they tell me to."

"Yes, Merry and I were unfortunate enough to stumble across that incident yesterday. It's a shame, such a young man." Chance remained silent about his relationship with Dr. Walters. Although the Chief of Police may have already told Reinhardt the victim was a friend of the magician, Chance played politics and didn't mention it. In order to gain access, he had to play his cards close to his chest. It was highly likely someone would say more to a disinterested magician in passing, than to one investigating the death of a friend.

"Young or not, he was one of my, and the country's, greatest engineers,"

Reinhardt said. "I can't tell you what he was working on, but we're talking real Buck Rogers stuff here. The kid was a genius. Now, I got contracts to fill and quotas to make but Research and Design is going off track and I don't need to tell you how important that is in wartime."

"Pardon my asking, Mr. Reinhardt, but aren't you getting any funding from the government?" Chance asked. "After all, it is wartime."

"We made the mistake of not starting business before Pearl Harbor got bombed," Reinhardt said. "Because of that, we were too late for a lot of government contracts. So we went into research and with each new design we gain a little more traction."

"Good to hear," Chance said and began meandering back to the car as the others followed. "It was a pleasure to meet you. Maybe we could have some coffee or perhaps a drink after the seminar tonight."

The two other men smilingly agreed, nodding their heads, shaking hands again and speaking in affirmations. After closing the doors to the car Merry and George remained silent until after they had turned their cruiser from the new pavement to the old.

"Looks like a close knit little town," Merry finally said.

"Maybe a little too close, Merry. I think we may need to check into the Mayor and Mr. Reinhardt's records."

"I can do even better," Merry said.

"Really?"

"Sure, easy. Did you get a look at 'Mayor MacDaffee's' hair? It's dyed. You want to find out anything in a small community like this, you go to the hairdresser."

"I have to admit, I wouldn't have thought of that."

Twenty minutes later Chance pulled the car into the town square of Hambone, South Carolina. It was a farming community just outside Burlington, its residents numbering around two-hundred-and-fifty people. He parked next to the cruiser in the only other parking space in front of the Hambone Inn. There was a barbershop in the hotel lobby and the building looked like it might have four rooms on top.

A man in a checkered suit and nauseously green, snap brim hat stepped out of the cruiser before Chance had finished parking. The silhouette of another man stood shadowed in back of the car.

"Glad you could find us," the man in the checkered suit said.

"How could I not?" Chance said. "Your suit was sending signals."

The man in the loud suit was none other than Joe Harper, one of the

Green Ghost's aides. Harper had spent the night on Chance's couch one time a few years back and never left. A perpetual bum, gambler, and arch-chiseler with an education in the lowest forms of downtown life, Harper also carried a gun in his shoulder rig and was always ready to aid the magician-criminologist.

"You already register here?" Chance nodded his head toward the hotel.

"Mr. Simms and Mr. Johnson."

"Not quite as obvious as Smith and Jones, but it'll have to do. It doesn't matter; you probably won't be spending too much time in your room, anyway. I want the two of you to follow us back to our hotel in Burlington. A certain green friend of ours is needed again, and I may need you to help sneak Glenn Saunders into my place."

"You take the high road, and I'll take the high road, too," Harper said, as if it were his motto.

"Oh, Joe, on the way back I want you to take note of the location of a construction site where they're doing some road work. There are about thirty oil drums stacked up behind a ditch on the side of the road. I may need you go by there later."

Harper shuddered at the words "you" and "construction site," afraid he might somehow be forced to work.

While George Chance and Merry kept the desk clerk at the hotel busy checking for messages and meeting their decidedly distracting guest, Mr. Joe Harper, another man slipped up the stairs behind them. The shadowy figure slid noiselessly down the hall to Chance's room and, putting a small lock-pick set to work for only a moment, let himself in the door.

The mysterious figure sat down on the bed, and it wasn't until the rest of the Green Ghost's merry band arrived that it became evident as to why Glenn Saunders' arrival had to remain secret. He was almost the exact double of George Chance.

Glenn Saunders was the one thing every magician needed, a duplicate. A magician himself, early in his career Saunders had met the world-famous Chance and been offered a unique proposition. He would become George Chance's double in exchange for the secrets of Chance's magic. Saunders would also act as Chance's alibi whenever the Green Ghost made an appearance. For if the underworld suspected for a moment that the famous magician-detective might be The Green Ghost, the attempts on his, and his loved ones' lives would never end.

Joe Harper pulled a chair from the desk, sat down, and pulled a cigarette from a silver case before holding it out to offer one to the others. Merry declined as she sat down on the bed next to Saunders. George Chance couldn't help but notice the cigarettes were his brand and wondered if he'd have any left when he got back home.

"If we're going to catch the murderer of Judd Walters, we're going to have to act fast," Chance said. "I've given you most of the details already, but I haven't had time to process it all. Merry, I need you to go to the hall of records. Check the local and state files for the city of Burlington, its relationship to Aerodyne Enterprises, and any other project that Stannard Reinhardt might be involved in."

"Aw, can't I go get my hair done?" Merry quipped, her eyes blinking in sarcastic remorse.

"Please do," Chance said, "after you check on those files. And don't be afraid to call the state agencies. In fact, you'll have to. Joe, I want you to drive me over to Fort Burlington, I have an appointment to meet with some of their staff and the U.S.O."

Harper shrugged his shoulders and nodded yes. Chance turned to face his double.

"Glenn, I'm afraid you're going to have to stay hidden until this afternoon. I'll give you a call when the coast is clear. Till then, I need you to develop the film I shot at Aerodyne Labs last night. I've already set up the darkroom equipment in the bathroom."

"Hope you've got rubber gloves, too," Saunders said. "People might notice if George Chance showed up at a party with dishpan hands."

"God forbid," Merry said.

Joe Harper tsk-tsked with his head.

Fort Burlington was a boot camp and officers school. The base was also rumored to house Top Secret research, specifically those projects approved by the government for Aerodyne industries, to eventually be coordinated with U.S. Defense. Chance noted the positions of the guards at the gate and realized the chances of sneaking on base were little to none.

After inspecting Chance's I.D., the guard in the booth told him that Colonel Shaughnessy would meet him at the auditorium and gave him directions to the building. However, after passing through the immediate courtyard, Chance told Joe Harper to park in front of the main office.

"But I thought this Colonel guy was going to meet you at the auditorium?" Harper said.

"He will, eventually," the man who was the Green Ghost said. "As tight as security is around here, it might be to our advantage to pretend we missed that little message and take a look around. I want you to come into the front office with me, in case I need a distraction. It might be our only opportunity."

George Chance planned to hide in plain sight. At the front desk, he and Harper introduced themselves by once again announcing they had an appointment with Colonel Shaughnessy.

"Oh, Mr. Chance," the uniformed man behind the counter said. "The Colonel is waiting for you at the auditorium."

"Really?" George Chance thumbed over his shoulder at Harper. "But, my friend here just got a message that we were supposed to stop here first and pick up some paperwork from Colonel Shaughnessy's office."

"Let me buzz his secretary."

By the time the corporal behind the desk had begun to dial the phone, Joe Harper had rested his elbows on the counter to become the feature attraction. George Chance was already making his way down a side hall. The secretary muttered into the phone and smiled awkwardly before speaking to Joe Harper again. Harper kept fidgeting uncomfortably, so much so, the man in uniform never noticed the missing magician.

"I'm sorry, sir, but Colonel Shaughnessy's secretary says she doesn't have anything for you."

"Doesn't have anything for me?" Joe Harper's beetle black eyes lit up just a little as he leaned back from the counter, as if insulted by the words. "Call again, corporal, I don't have time for this kind of runaround. We're trying to put on a show for our boys here!" Harper estimated he could keep the corporal busy with his questions and complaints for a good ten minutes, after that the boss was on his own.

Chance wasted no time twisting his way down a hall and into an empty office, most likely used for interviews. The magician detective found a map of the installation in the top drawer. The buildings were numbered on the map with department headings listed by the numbers underneath. Two buildings were labeled research. One had the letters "A.I.D.P." Chance hoped that stood for Aerodyne Industries Defense Program. It was all he had to go on.

Locating the auditorium on the map, he found the research lab relatively close to it. He'd have to wander a bit out of the way, but might be able to do it if he pretended to be lost.

That's when he remembered he'd left Joe Harper to divert the secretary's attention. Quickly, he strode back down the hall. Harper was an ex-circus

"The Colonel is waiting ...at the auditorium."

hawker and pitchman and perhaps the best diversion in the world, but in this case, if he did his job too well, then Chance and Harper might be given a guide to the auditorium. And the last thing The Green Ghost wanted was guide.

"I tell you, Corporal Wylie, Mr. Chance has been shipping paper back and forth to the colonel for months now. And if the colonel tells the world famous Mr. George Chance those papers are on his desk..."

Chance grabbed Joe Harper by the arm, made a motion toward the front door with his head.

"...well, we'll just have to talk to the colonel about that," Harper finished, smiling and tipping his nauseatingly green hat.

Chance could hear the secretary's sigh of relief as the wizard of welshers turned toward the door and they left.

Outside, Chance and Harper wandered northwest, to the right of and just behind the auditorium. With the summer trees blooming and the several buildings scattered across the base, there was just enough cover that they wouldn't have to worry about Colonel Shaughnessy spotting them from the auditorium. The two men followed a winding lane to a building about the size of a small schoolhouse.

Two guards stood at attention, posted outside the door. Hedges lined the building, but there were no gates or booths to be herded through.

While Chance lumbered in the shadows of a few trees, Joe Harper went back to work. Stumbling directly up to the guards, he pretended to search for his I.D. then quickly spilt all the change out of his pockets, making sure to spread the coins over a fare sized part of ground. After a minute, he'd muttered enough complaints about being a guest that one of the guards bent over to help him pick up the change. The other guard remained at attention.

Chance reached into one of his many pockets, and pulled out a wind-up children's toy he'd picked up at the five-and-dime. Marketed as the "Wild Spider," the silver disk had two long legs that wound up and spun like a propeller to send it skittering wildly across the ground, bouncing off walls and jumping everything else in its path. Chance wound the toy up and hurled it through the air, where it landed with magnet-like precision on the edge of the post where Harper and the guards stood. The silvery "spider" hit the sidewalk, reeled away from the men and into the hedges in front of the building like a robotic wild animal.

The guard remaining at attention jumped to see what it was. The other guard kept picking up change, but watched in confusion as his partner ran to scour the hedges. Joe Harper kept harping, making concentration impossible. Meanwhile, a shadowy figure in a green suit slid behind the hedges on the other side of the building and stole through the door.

Once inside, Chance turned and strode down the hall as if he belonged there. He had no idea of the security set-up, but he knew that acting like you belonged somewhere was half the battle. Of course, if someone were to call him out, he would have to pretend to be lost.

There was nobody inside. Nothing. Chance walked down the empty halls opening doors, looking into offices and labs with nothing in them. At the back of the building he found one office with a desk. There were invoices on the table for basic chemistry parts, beakers and the like, electrical components, metallurgy equipment, and a number of scientific sounding devices George Chance was not familiar with.

A desk covered with invoices. But no equipment. An entire building dedicated to research in wartime with no equipment in it. It didn't make sense.

Chance made his way back out the front door quickly. The guards were back on alert, but it looked like Harper was pumping them for information. Chance simply walked behind one of the guards like he belonged there and ended up standing next to Harper, all so nonchalantly that neither soldier even noticed.

"Joe! There you are!" Chance grabbed him by the shoulder. "Thought I'd lost you."

Harper turned as if he'd been waiting for Chance to arrive. Introductions were made. The guards got autographs.

It was only a few hundred yards to the auditorium office, where Colonel Dale Shaughnessy was all business with Chance from the first. The colonel reviewed Chance's planned presentation on crooked games of chance. George Chance assured him he'd given the presentation on a half-dozen other bases and had a host of props, from rigged roulette wheels to crooked crap tables, to keep the men entertained and informed. Chance had to wait for the proper moment to bring up the murder of Judd Walters.

"I was wondering, Colonel," Chance said, towards the end of the meeting. "An employee of Aerodyne Industries was found dead in town yesterday. It's no secret that Fort Burlington was scheduled to coordinate research between Aerodyne and the government. I was wondering what you might think, or, perhaps, if you had any suspicions of your own."

"Ah, Judd Walters. I heard all about it. Sad, he was such an enthusiastic young man." The colonel paused for a moment as if thinking. "At least, when I first met him."

"I'd think losing a little enthusiasm while trying to conquer new fields of science is pretty common."

"It is, it is...but the boy seemed to be doing everything on his own. Government contracts were contingent on Aerodyne's developments, and while he knew his wind-to-wing resistance research was valid, it had yet to be proven. It was a situation designed to build tension in a young man like that, like waiting for the gunfight in a western movie. Just waiting, and never getting the chance to prove yourself."

"I understood the government was working with, funding Aerodyne."

"The government has a financial interest, stock and payment on work orders, all of it used for research and development. I've seen a few large pallets of material move into Aerodyne's laboratories, but not so much as to build a research facility on. Seems like they're the last to get their orders filled, probably all the confusion on the home front over the war. The big money's going for armory, ships and field weapons. Proven products and tactics."

"As it should, I suppose," Chance said. "Still, I don't think that would have driven anyone to cut his head off."

The major gave the comment no reaction, other than to pull a cigar out of his pocket and clip the end with a pocket knife. Pulling a silver-plated lighter out his pocket, he ran the flame around one end of the cigar as he spoke.

"One of the reasons the United States puts Army bases where they do, besides the price of real estate, is so we can train the behavior of our men off-base, as well as on. Burlington is that typical town. Yes, we have a few crooked gambling establishments and dishonest roadhouses, but so do towns all over America. Burlington is not the heart of spy country, you can count on that. More likely, in a town like this, I'm willing to bet it was a crime of passion. People in small towns get caught up in the strangest affairs, there's so little else to do."

"No offense, Colonel, but Judd never struck me as the impulsive type. He was the kind of guy that was always working on something, or just went fishing."

"Well, whatever he caught ripped his head off. Just between you and me, the whole Aerodyne project may be so top secret it's barely close to existing. All we really know here is that it involves aircraft design. I suppose the ones that would really know are in Washington, and we won't have any word from them till this evening."

On the way out Chance turned to Harper.

"I'm afraid the colonel might have a point, Joe. Judd Walters was a fisherman, he had loads of patience. He was used to waiting. So I don't think ordinary project delays would have dampened his enthusiasm. It is possible it could be something as common as a crime of passion. Unless, of course, he found there was no chance of landing the fish he wanted."

"You mean like maybe the project's goal had changed?" Joe Harper said as he slid behind the wheel of the rental car.

"Exactly, but in a case of espionage, an agent isn't going to just surgically lop off somebody's head. Something like that would only call unwanted attention to the case. Joe, I need you to get me a sample of that 'sealant' the city is using on the tarmac, now. With the feds moving in, we may not have much time. At this point it's all just a bunch of puzzle pieces, but something about those oil drums keeps digging at me. Should they be guarded you can either pretend to be part of the construction project or use your talents with the blackjack."

Harper nodded at Chance and placed a hand on the sap he kept handy in his coat pocket. Chance considered it highly unlikely Harper would even pretend to work. Harper liked being sneaky. And he liked using a sap.

"Unfortunately, I have to get back to the hotel and match our notes with the information everybody else has collected. You'll have to walk back, Joe. I don't want anybody knowing what we're up to. It should be less than a mile through the woods."

Harper winced. Even if he only had to sap a guy, he'd still have to perform some sort of physical exertion. The Master of Mooch pulled over about a quarter mile past the construction site, which, while a good strategic move, also meant he might not have to walk as far back to the hotel. Chance took the cruiser's wheel and sped back to the hotel, facts whirling in his head as tried to make sense of the case.

Back at the Hotel Burlington, Chance was greeted in his room by a haggard looking Glenn Saunders who, of course, looked like a rather haggard George Chance. Chance's double had spent the morning in the improvised darkroom. With only the one window open in the bathroom there wasn't a lot of ventilation, and since Saunders couldn't simply open the window and stick his head out, it appeared the fumes had gotten to him.

"Little bit of cabin fever there, buddy?" Chance handed his fellow magician a sandwich and a soda they'd picked up on the road. Saunders pried the bag open and swallowed half the sandwich in one bite.

"Just getting a little light headed, boss," Saunders said. "I developed all that film and I mean ALL that film. Guy was writing a book."

"Anything stand out?" Chance sat down behind the desk and began to rifle through a pile of pictures.

"I don't know. I couldn't exactly develop them in order. The notebook looks like a journal of sorts, his ups and downs in the program, a bunch of invoices with due dates, and past due dates. The pictures of the pictures were the hardest to develop. Mostly just corners of buildings, sidewalks, some windows…"

"Windows, eh?" Chance narrowed one eye and considered the amount of film still hanging like curtains from the shower rod. "Let me see the window stuff."

"Sure." Saunders pulled through the photos piled on the desk and handed a few of them to Chance. "You mind if I go outside, and get some air for a minute? I got to see some daylight."

"Sure, just don't wander too far." Saunders let himself out as Chance rifled through the photographs. A few minutes later, there was a tap on the door and Merry White let herself into the room.

"How do you like my hair, darlin'? You paid for it, you know."

"Hard to tell under that hat." Chance looked up at her, smiling. "I'll never understand why women pay a fortune to get their hair done and then hide it under a jumble of ribbon and flaps."

"At least I didn't make you pay for the hat." Merry dropped her bag and a briefcase on the bed. "Which, they seemed to like a lot over at the Hall of Records."

"Any problems?" Chance asked.

"Other than a few enlisted wolves? None. None for Aerodyne Enterprises, the City of Burlington and, or, any of its officers and business elite, either. I even called the state comptroller. Everything seems to be on the up and up between Aerodyne and the State."

"What did the hairdresser have to say?"

"Like I said, the mayor dyes his hair. Evidently, so do some of the other men in town. Mrs. Pritzker, that's the hairdresser's name, was complaining that the local barber had started stocking hair dye over the counter and killed her business with the mayor."

Chance stared into space with his hand on his chin a moment. It was hard to tell if he was thinking or just waiting.

"She also said that the city reps and Aerodyne spent a lot of their time together. Chief Deighton, Reinhardt, and MacAfee, they're a tight knit group."

"Yes, it seems so. Do you think you could use your feminine charms to find out who the barber's dye customers are? I've got an odd hunch."

"I'm on it, darlin'," Merry said.

"And instead of the comptroller, could you do me a favor and call up some of the actual vendors on those files? I'd like to see what they have to say. While we're at it, see if you can't dig up a copy of the road paving contract? I need to know where the money is."

Merry pulled out a list and wrote down her mission. Chance continued to speak without moving his head, still deep in thought.

Merry grabbed her bag and they headed for the door. Chance continued to shuffle through the pictures, separating the actual photos from the written journal.

The journal pages weren't numbered, so Chance simply began reading at one point, then trying to find the next page that fit. An hour later he almost had it. Dr. Judd Walters' notes were full of complaints about ordered products not arriving and when they did, they were deficient. It all came down to one complaint. "How can I perform real experiments without the equipment? I am so tired of 'hurry up and wait!'"

Was it merely the complaint of an overzealous scientist, or was there really something impeding the progress of whatever he was working on?

He was staring at a picture of cracked concrete in a stone wall when it hit him. They looked like insurance photos. Chance had seen many an insurance investigator sent out to take pictures just like these, flawed buildings and cracks in the sidewalk. The only thing missing were the car photos. Usually, there were pictures of cars in accident investigations. This one didn't have any.

Chance could only come to one conclusion. Dr. Judd Walters had been investigating Aerodyne Industries, his own company. Chance kept staring at the picture of a broken window.

"Curiouser and curiouser," he mumbled to himself.

The door opened and Glenn Saunders sauntered back into the hotel room with his arm around Joe Harper. Saunders cheeks were ruddy with summer heat, while Harper appeared to be melting in his suit, a coffee can smeared with oil hanging from his left hand.

"Look who wandered out of the woods while I was taking a walk," Saunders said. "Of course with that sport coat on I spotted him a half-mile before he saw me."

Harper shrugged his way out from under Saunders arm, sat on the bed and extended the oily coffee can toward Chance, who grabbed it and took a sample with the tip of his finger.

"Looks like old oil to me, boss. Black, old oil." Joe lit a cigarette the second the can was out of his hands. It bobbed up and down between his lips as he spoke.

"Huh." Chance rubbed the oil between his thumb and forefinger. "Maybe there's some sort of chemical reaction when it settles into the tarmac. I'll have to take a look at it with the chemistry set. Luckily, we already practically have a crime lab in the washroom. " Chance grabbed a square leather case off the floor and rose from his chair in one movement, treading toward the bath.

"Reminds me of a story this friend of mine told me, about how some Gypsies travelled around in the hill country." Joe Harper had begun talking to George Sanders as if George Chance had never left the room. "These Gypsies, they'd claim they were going to fix a tarmac road, then pour oil all over it so the old road looked like new. A few weeks later all that new looking road would just wash away in the rain."

"Really?" Glenn Saunders said, sitting behind the desk and picking some pictures.

"Really," Chance's voice echoed in the affirmative from the bathroom. "It's a common confidence game played on farmers and ranchers, mostly because by the time they're aware the crime has been committed the criminal is already out of the state."

"You think somebody would have killed Judd Walters to cover up a Gypsy oil scam?" Saunders said.

I seriously doubt it," Chance answered. "There's a big difference between going to the electric chair and serving three to five on a fraud charge. Plus, to pull such a stunt on an entire community would increase cost, and they'd have to have an incredible exit strategy managed out. It's just not worth the few hundred dollars profit the suspect would make. And, there's no way they could ever show their face in the community... heck, the state...ever again."

"Still looks like a scam to me," Joe Harper said.

Because it is," Chance stuck his head out of the bathroom and held up a test tube full of muck. "At least as far as preliminary tests go. What we've got here appears to be oil sludge, mud, and maybe a little sugar to hold it to the road. Nothing in the mixture appears to be sealing, or even drying."

"Used oil," Saunders said. "Now, that's just lowdown crazy. First rain, the ditches will be full of cars."

"Speaking of sanity," Chance said. "I hope Merry didn't stop to buy

Chance….held up a test tube full of muck.

another hat. We're not going to know anything, until we find out what the vendors have to say about those invoices."

"And who's dyeing their hair?" Harper asked.

"And who's dyeing their hair..." There was a moment of silence where George Chance appeared to be in thought. He opened one of his suitcases and removed a can of pomade, a pair of horn rim glasses and a set of false teeth.

"Glenn," Chance said, handing his double the glasses. "I may need you to put on part of show tonight. Slick your hair back, part it in the middle and put on these. With the teeth and glasses, I don't think anybody will notice the resemblance. You can ride with me in the car."

Chance had no qualms about letting Glenn Saunders take his place on stage. Saunders was more than professional. And, it would give Chance the alibi he needed to cover for The Green Ghost. Two hours till show time.

While the auditorium at Fort Burlington filled to the rafters with people to see the world famous magician, Chance stood behind the stage curtains, parting them with one hand and peering out onto the crowd. George Chance had introduced Glenn Saunders as a manager, and with the combined skills of two illusionists disguising him, no one had been the wiser. Saunders waited in the dressing room, removing his disguise. In the beginning he'd almost been George Chance's exact double, so he was relieved to see his smiling face in the mirror. Saunders had always considered impersonation part of the world of magic, and was proud to be in on Chance's little act.

An array of oversized gambling paraphernalia sat on a table in the middle of the stage, a craps block and a pool table on either side. Chance knew he had a captive audience, many of them avid gamblers, but he still felt the need to perform a few tricks just to keep it interesting. Colonel Shaugnessy stepped up to the podium for the introduction.

"Gentleman, the Fort Burlington United States Army Base is proud to present George Chance's Honest Gamble, or as we used to call it, How Not To Be A Sucker!" The crowd chuckled. "I want your full and undivided attention, men. Remember this is just a seminar, no gambling in the aisles. "

A mild wave of laughter went through the crowd, then the soldiers went nuts, standing, yelling and whistling for the magical George Chance. The magician, in evening dress with no hat, had to bow for several minutes until the crowd finally got quiet. Then even quieter. Chance had mastered the art of building tension a long time ago.

He strode briskly to the center table and picked up the pair of oversized dice. Balancing the two-foot square blocks by their corners, one on each hand, Chance spun to face the microphone, his coattails waving behind him.

"Gentleman, raise your hand if you know how to spot a set of loaded dice?" Some of the men's hands almost went up. Somebody laughed hard, but for the most part nobody raised their hand.

"That's right, men. Anybody that's won a dice game in the last week just realized they better not raise their hand, and everybody that's lost a game is looking to see who else raised theirs."

The crowd chuckled at their own reactions.

Chance proceeded to pull weighted faux jewels from the giant dice, and passed them around to the soldiers in the crowd. Then he arranged them on the dice so he could roll a two, two out of three times. The men nodded in understanding, as Chance proceeded to hold up a small black device with wires trailing from either end of it.

"Anybody know what this is? Anybody willing to raise their hand?"

None of the soldiers did.

"This little device is the friend and winning odds maker in many a crooked roadhouse and saloon. It is an electromagnet. It can be used in almost any gamble where there's metal involved, and that's mostly in dice and roulette. Watch."

Chance pulled up a tablecloth on the center table, which was tilted slightly so the crowd could see. Chance then proceeded to announce he would roll a five with his giant dice, and did.

"By moving the jeweled weights around I can also adjust which side will receive the most magnet pull." Chance moved some weights and proceeded to roll a two, three times in a row.

After pulling a disconnected roulette wheel from the table, he began to show the men how the ball could be controlled by electromagnets underneath the wheel. For the next forty minutes, he educated them in the ways of leaning roulette tables and rigged table mechanisms.

Chance predicted his silver ball would land on the number three. It did, and the crowd broke into applause as Chance wound up juggling three tiny roulette balls. He tossed them in the air and they stuck to the electromagnet mounted on the wall behind him.

The crowd was cheering when Merry White arrived, waving frantically from the backstage. The moment Chance saw her he set up the action onstage for the intermission.

"Of course, a real magician doesn't need magnets," Chance announced, and a card, the ace of spades, appeared in his hand. Several pieces of fruit sat on a table a good twenty yards from where Chance stood. Holding the card sideways, Chance flung it like a spinning knife through the air, and the ace of spades chopped the top off of a piece of squash. Chance threw three more cards, and all three stuck into the side of a watermelon.

That's when it hit Chance. If a playing card can be thrown hard enough to slice through fruit, what about a pane of glass? And he suddenly realized what had killed Judd Walters.

"I'll be right back after a short intermission, and then we'll take a look at a few more card tricks!" The soldiers applauded as the curtains closed. Chance ran to the wings where Merry and Joe Harper stood waiting.

"The federal government has paid out cash for five different vendors, and of those five, four are still waiting to get paid by Aerodyne Laboratories," Merry blurted out.

"And Stannard Reinhardt dyes his hair, too," Chance said.

"How did you know?" Merry's eyes went wide.

"Because he's pulling one of the oldest confidence games in the book, the magic wallet."

"What?" Merry said.

"The magic wallet. Con men looking to wheedle investors into giving them money would pretend to lose a wallet where the victim would find it. The wallet was planted full of money and whatever sort of papers the con men wanted the victim to see, a letter from the president for instance. The con man's mark, believing the fake paperwork, would see nothing but a clean investment, approved by the paperwork in the wallet and the con artist's obvious wealth. The mark invests with the con man, and the con man disappears. Anybody seen Reinhardt here tonight?"

"Come to think of it, no," Joe Harper said. "The mayor and his crowd are all here, hanging out with the colonel, but our friend Reinhardt seems to be noticeably absent."

"He said he was going to meet with the federal agents when they arrived," Mary said. "And they're arriving tonight, remember?"

"What he said and what he's going to do are exact opposites," Chance said. "It's my guess that he had an exit strategy from the beginning, he's just had to speed it up. Merry, tell Glenn Saunders he'll have to finish the act. Joe, come with me. We've got a con man to catch."

Two headlights glimmered from the west like fireflies in the distance. The fireflies extinguished themselves, but the hum of a sedan's engine continued to drift down the darkened lane. Joe Harper pulled the car over across the street and left the engine running. The Green Ghost pulled on his gloves, and spoke as he reached for the door.

"Joe, we're on a deadline here, time is of the essence. If we don't crack this case right now, the man responsible for Judd Walters' death is going to escape. And even if our quarry hasn't already skipped town, federal agents will be knocking down the door at any second. I'm afraid the FBI may have a few too many questions for the Green Ghost, even if they do need him to solve this case." Chance reached for the door handle then paused and turned toward Harper.

"I'm surprised the feds aren't here already. I'll need you signal me the second a car, any car, parks near the house. Part of the Green Ghost's power is his mystery, and I can't afford to be taken in, even if it's just for questioning."

"I'll whistle a few bird calls," Harper spoke through his cigarette. "If you should suddenly hear a very aggressive robin, you'll know somebody's coming."

The Ghost pulled the brim of his crusher hat down low, drifted out the door and melted into the darkness.

Stannard Reinhardt's house stood on a hill just to the east of town. Bigger than most every other house in town, it was easy to spot, despite the murky shadows and mossy tree line in front. Reinhardt stood in the kitchen with his bags packed, sweating and looking at his watch. 8:00 PM, the FBI men would be arriving at the airport where he was supposed to meet them. Of course, he wouldn't.

The bags he'd packed were full of bank books with phony names and accounts in three different states. Altogether it added up to about two-hundred thousand dollars, directly from the United States Treasury. He picked up his bags and headed for the back door, cursing.

Everything would have been fine, if Walters just hadn't been so damned headstrong, so curious. Reinhardt had pulled this con twice before under different names, setting himself up as a respectable businessman, finding a solid, well-known citizen to front his company so it would look respectable to investors.

The con worked so well, because he had a guy like Judd Walter's fronting for him. Walters had never suspected that in the end he'd have to take the blame. No, instead Walters had just kept shuttling around the labs, checking invoices, and making phone calls. It would only have been a matter of time until he found out he was the patsy. Still, Reinhardt hadn't wanted him killed. It had been an accident, and it had forced him to play his hand. He'd take the car to New York, and disappear again. Maybe try this con out West somewhere where the people weren't quite as well informed.

Reinhardt grabbed the handles of both his suitcases and made his way out the back door. He left the porch light off and didn't bother to lock the door behind him. It wasn't as if he planned on coming back.

But, Reinhardt wasn't ready for the demon on the back steps.

Out of the blackness two eyes like black holes appeared in the center of an emerald glow. Then a figure with a green death's head face emerged as if from a mist, and black, dead lips skinned themselves in a smile revealing the rictus grin of a corpse.

Reinhardt dropped his bags on the porch and stood staring at the Green Ghost, his mouth open, his entire face wide.

"Stannard Reinhardt! You are guilty of murder." The Ghost's voice peeled like cracking wood as came closer. "Then again, your name is about as real as your construction supplies." The Ghost chuckled to himself, the cackle of a madman.

Reinhardt shaking, finally forced out the words, "I-I didn't kill him...It was a...an accident."

"You might as well have signed the death warrant. Judd Walters lost his head at Aerodyne's laboratories due to your inferior materials. One of the sub-par windows blew out of the side of the lab's wind tunnel and cut his head off. Rather than report it to the authorities and call attention to your crimes, you decided it would be easier if it looked like espionage. Then, if the feds were called into solve the case, you'd still have time to skip town."

"It was an accident," Reinhardt repeated, gasping.

"No, it was a plan. You just hadn't planned on hanging around to see its effect. Con men call it the "magic wallet" game. You just used Walters to build your false front instead of some paperwork."

Reinhardt stood as if he were freezing in the summer heat, shivering. His bottom jaw fluttered as if he was trying not to let his teeth chatter.

"You hired Judd Walters as a front. With his good name, you knew you'd have no shortage of investors to Aerodyne Enterprises. But you weren't counting on Pearl Harbor. Pearl pulled the U.S Military into the deal; you weren't happy about that, but it was hard to stop once you saw all that federal money piling up. You'd probably already set an exit date and intended Walters to take the fall for you, when the glass in the wind tunnel cut his head off." The Ghost held up the piece of glass he'd picked up on his first visit to Aerodyne's wind tunnel, and pointed it at Reinhardt.

"It was hard to clean up all that blood in the lab wasn't it? I mean, a beheading, I can only imagine the mess. But you missed this piece of tempered glass, tempered proving it came from the wind tunnel. There was a blood sample on it, the same blood type as Judd Walters, B-positive."

"It was an accident, I swear!" Reinhardt begged. "He was adjusting one of the wings on one of his rockets, and the glass blew out of the side of the tunnel. I needed time, and the only way I could think of was to relocate the body and then close up shop as quickly as possible."

"But you got greedy. Even with the coffers full and Aerodyne's warehouse empty, the road construction con at the last moment was just too easy to pass up. And it's a short ride from grifter construction swindles to the magic wallet con. If you hadn't been in the middle of such a blatant confidence game, I never would have suspected."

Reinhardt stood with hand in his coat pocket. There was a moment of silence and the still air stiffened. Tension hung over it like the splint on a wound. The quiet became taught. But George Chance had mastered the art of building tension a long time ago.

Reinhardt's hand pulled free of his pocket revealing a .45 automatic. A knife flew from the Green Ghosts hand even as the swindler raised the barrel. Reinhardt fired from the hip, and the Green Ghost's dagger went spinning into the shadows. Whatever Reinhardt's real name was, he was a good shot.

But when Reinhardt looked back up, the Green Ghost was gone. As good a shot as the deadly swindler was, he still had to see what he was aiming at. Chance had simply switched off the tiny green light on his tiepin and let the rest of his wardrobe do the work for him; the dark green of the Ghost's outfit was perfect for blending in the shadows of the outdoors.

"No, you can't do this to me," Reinhardt yelled and whimpered at the same time. His body shook with tremors, his knees wavered and the waving shadows trembled across the yard. "You..." He waved the gun around in the air, squinting with one eye. "You..." His bottom lip trembled. His breathing went from erratic to almost none. "Are you even there?"

The chirruping of crickets and frogs was his only answer. Then an odd bird call sounded in the distance, like something had invaded a robin's nest. The con man's head shuddered and jerked on his neck from side to side. He inhaled in short breaths and took confidence in his gun, gripping it tightly.

A smiling green skull-face popped out of the night directly in front of him and sighed. Reinhardt dropped the gun.

He bent over to pick it up and something kicked him behind the knees. He fell on the porch and jumped back to his feet, failing to retrieve the gun and spinning around in circles, waving his hands in the air trying to feel what he couldn't see.

Then the face lit up in front of him again, and the con man felt the point of the Green Ghost's knife on his throat.

Reinhardt focused on the drifting light eking through the windows of the house behind him. His whole body jerked erect and he bolted for the back door, tripping over his luggage. He felt the green glow behind him as much as he saw it. Stumbling to his feet, he heard the Green Ghost's steely whisper.

"Confession is good for the soul, con man. Tell them everything."

"No. Wha? Wh-who?" Reinhardt rattled, as he tried to gain enough balance to crawl through the door. Then he saw the grinning skull, and felt the barrel of the gun against the top of his head.

"Whoever asks. Tell them. The truth. Remember, I'll be watching you."

Reinhardt screamed. His nails scraped at the boards, as his feet slid churning beneath him. Clawing at the screen door he wrenched it open, and yanked the door inside almost off its hinges. He pressed the light switch inside the door, and sprinted for the front door, until he hit the hallway, where he reached to press the light switch again. He even turned the lights on in the living room before he burst out the front door, screaming.

"I did it! I did it!" Reinhardt wailed, and kept repeating as he sprinted onto the front porch.

The two FBI agents on the steps already had their guns drawn, but it made no difference. Reinhardt barreled right into them. One of the agents went down swinging at the con man's head with his service revolver. The other punched Reinhardt in the jaw with a roundhouse swing. The con man hit the ground barely conscious.

"What the hell is going on here?" the agent who had been knocked down said.

"I'm still not sure yet, Larry," the agent in a snap brim hat said. "But this guy looks kind of familiar."

"Wait a minute," the younger agent said, getting up and dusting off his knees. "That last batch of teletypes we got before we flew here. Looks like he could be one of them...except something's different."

"Well, I'll be," the agent in the snap brim hat said. "Looks like one James

Fleming, alias Cornell Straight, alias about a dozen others, dyed his hair red this time. Who would've thought?"

"I did it," Reinhardt mumbled, almost unconscious.

"We know you did, Jim," the younger agent said, bending the con man's prostrate figure forward to slap the cuffs on. "We know you did."

"I still have some questions," the agent in the snap brim hat said.

"Me too." The younger agent stuck his head inside the front door and glanced at the interior of the house. "Like why'd he have to switch all the lights on before he came running through the house? He scared of the dark or something?"

THE END

RIPPING THE ROCKETMAN

For my money, G. T. Fleming Roberts was one of the greatest pulp hero writers ever. While he never had a long run on a major character like Doc Savage or The Shadow, Roberts seemed to touch every other pulp hero on the planet, going so far as to write the last of the greatest, Captain Zero. He had it almost down to a formula, and you can see it especially in the Black Hood stories. One of the reasons the original Green Ghost stories were so great was that by the end of the Ghost's run in Thrilling Mystery, he had to share the magazine. Robert's Green Ghost stories became sharp and fast because they didn't have to be padded to fit a novelette length. So, when Ron Fortier gave me the opportunity to write a Green Ghost story, I leapt at it.

See, The Ghost didn't always deal with super villains trying to take over the world. He quite often took on forgery rings, swindlers, and con men. And as anybody who's read any of my Bagman stories, I love the subject of confidence man. But what kind of con would it be? How could I get you, the reader, interested on that first page?

Well, a headless body usually gets somebody's attention. But I couldn't just have some maniac chopping off heads. This was a Green Ghost story, not The Spider. Something about that connection made me think about a headless body with no blood. Now that's a mystery.

So how did he lose his head? Well, The Ghost stories did appear during World War Two, and that led me to think of aviation. After all, even if we didn't know it, that era was the beginning of our missile program. So, I had a scientist in aviation that would get his head cut off. Still, there were the same two questions. How did he lose his head, and why?

He couldn't just have it chopped off, that's too easy, not enough mystery. That's when I remembered how pine needles are found embedded in trees after tornadoes. Anything moving fast enough can be a deadly weapon. And, what could slice a guy's head off faster than glass?

So where did the glass come from? Duh, a wind tunnel, they still use them to study aerodynamics and it would have been the height of technology at the time.

I had the victim, I had the method. I just didn't have an original motive. Sure, the villain could be a Nazi spy, but I didn't really remember The Ghost taking on spies, and it just seemed too easy.

Given my background with confidence men in The Bagman books, the immediate answer was: It's was a con. But which one? There's a wonderful book called Hustlers and Con Men by J. Robert Nash, and I highly recommend it to anybody that' s interested in the history and evolution of the con. I didn't even have to browse through the book, because the Magic Wallet immediately came to mind. The thing about the magic wallet is that it's a con that's still evolving to this day. You know those e-mails you get from Nigerian Kings telling you if you send them all your personal information you'll get a million bucks? That intro is right out of the Magic Wallet.

Now the original idea for the Magic Wallet was to leave paperwork around for the victim to find on their own, and make the victim think you had big bucks and were respectable. Needless to say, it has evolved enough since then that using another unknowing, respectable victim to front the con is practically an industry today. I regret to say that charity organizations and political action committees still fall for this sort of thing all the time.

Now I had a mystery. The dead rocket engineer and his entire organization would be the victims of The Magic Wallet.

I'd read a Ghost story where he was touring the country, protecting our military from crooked games of chance and used that to start, then went right to the body.

Then I just started playing. I love Merry White's character. There was always a bit of The Thin Man movie dialogue between her and The Ghost which I've always loved and then somehow the hair dye idea came in, and I decided to use that for a red herring to make the reader think the Mayor did it. Joe Harper, World War Two's greatest "slacker" practically wrote himself.

The hardest part of this story was getting the reader the info without just having all of The Ghost's crew come into the hotel room and tell him what's going on. I did my best to get them outdoors and into the action. I sincerely hope you and Mr. Fleming-Roberts approve.

B. C(hris). Bell - is the author and creator of the*Tales of The Bagman* series. The second Volume, *The Bagman vs. The World's Fair* is the latest. Bell has written some dozen pulp adventure novellas for heroes ranging from *The Avenger to Secret Agent X,* many of them for Airship 27 Productions. Bell's slipstream novel, *Bipolar Express,* made the 2012 Horror Writer Association's Reading List. His novella *Sometimes They Pay in Bullets,* a tribute to Black Mask Author Paul Cain, is also now available in the upcoming *Black Fedora* Anthology from Pro Se Press. Bell lives in Chicago, naturally, with his wife. You can follow B.C. on Facebook at: [https://www.facebook.com/B.C.Bell.Writes?ref=tn_tnmn] and On his Amazon Page at: [http://www.amazon.com/B.C.-Bell/e/B002QTUC2E]

MURDER IN SOUND EFFECTS
Erwin K. Roberts

George Chance sputtered, "What do you mean you've booked me on a radio show?!"

Tiny Tim Terry relit his five cent cigar before he replied, "That's right. I bumped into Walt Gibert yesterday. He's headed up to Maine to pound out some more Shade stories. He tipped me to an offer he's had."

"Magic on the radio? What am I supposed to do? Have the announcer say, 'Chandu gestures hypnotically...' before the sound effect of an elephant appearing?"

"You forget about Walter's past, George. He was the Great Gandall's biographer. Not to mention an expert on the history of magic. Like you, he's friends with all the major names and a lot of the up and coming ones working today. The folks at *Who's In Town?* wanted him to come on once or twice a month. He'd talk about who's performing and where. If needed, he'd tell stories about famous magicians. Nowadays you're more in town than he is. If we play our cards right, we can get a formal plug for your New York School of Magic every time you show up. What'd you say to that?"

Sunday night, two weeks later, Chance sat in front of a microphone wondering if he needed to have his head examined. Sure, he had a stack of notes in front of him, but still he felt nervous. In the past he'd been interviewed by radio show hosts or reporters as he toured. Those, mostly, were one-on-one affairs. This show had all the guests in a make-believe "parlor." He would be asked for a report on the state of magic in the region. Once all the regulars and guests, like him, reported a general discussion would begin. Who knew where that might lead.

As the studio clock approached the hour Lamar Richards, *Who's In Town's* host, stopped his low chat with Herbert Johnston, the Producer. As Johnston exited for the control room, Richards addressed each guest in turn, starting on his left. Mr. Broadway, New York Comet columnist Walt Whitley, was the only one Chance had actually met before. Miss Film, show name for Abby Francis, did well as an actress, until the studios all moved west. She still remained a well informed fan of the industry. Known as Tom Club, Thomas McKewen apparently visited every venue from Long Island, to Harlem, to Jersey. Da Sport, born Phil Martinelli, once caught for the Brooklyn Dodgers. Before they sat down George heard him mumble irritably to Miss Film about having to mention an upcoming ice show. Air Waver, Chance could not remember the real name of the man who sat next to him. He came on now and then to report on events where the public could actually see stars of radio shows in person. On George's other side sat Arthur Raymond, now appearing in an off Broadway production of *All Quiet on the Western Front*. Off behind them Murray "Splat" Robbins tested the weird collection of stuff that produced the show's sound effects.

"One minute," called out Lamar Richards. "Splat, put down that kazoo. Starting with Walt, go around the table and say your names as a last mike check." He paused after they complied. "How'd that sound Ralph? We ready?"

Engineer Ralph Owens' voice boomed out of a speaker above the control room window. "Sounded good, Lamar. Fifteen seconds... Ten seconds... Five..."

The speaker cut out. George, the host, and some of the others watched through the window as Ralph finished the countdown on his fingers. Then the prerecorded introduction to the show came up.

Chance recognized the up tempo voiceover as the work of the much in demand Ed Jeffries. "Live from Rockefeller Center, find out *Who's In Town!* Presented by The Wonderful Bakery line of cookies and snacks. Everybody loves something Wonderful as they listen to the radio. Tonight's broadcast is going out live to the whole region on the Lamont Network. Now let's find out *Who's In Town!* Take it away Lamar Richards!"

"Good evening to you all..."

A veteran of live stage performances, George Chance felt himself relax. He listened as Richards bantered a bit with the regulars. Next came their reports. Then he was introduced. As he spoke without reference to his notes Chance saw Arthur Raymond draw himself up for his turn. Everybody here knew that this broadcast would increase the B.I.C. of a little known production. Cance almost stumbled over a word when the unflattering definition of B.I.C. (Butts In Chairs) flashed through his mind. Then his report ended.

"Thank you, George," said Lamar Richards brightly. "Let me remind anybody naughty enough to tune in late that we have just heard from master magician George Chance. We hope this will be the first of many visits. Now, let's start the discussion with..."

Splat's ringing of a doorbell interrupted.

"Well now," continued Richard, "seems we have another guest. Rupert!

Will you please answer the door."

With a hard soled leather shoe on each hand Splat used a large square of parquet flooring to walk the completely imaginary butler across the room. Slipping off one shoe Splats reached for the two foot by three foot wood door set in the studio wall. He opened the door with one hand while somehow creating a creaking sound with something in the other.

Richards positively beamed, "Why Arthur Raymond, you did make it."

"That's right, Mr. Richards. But I can't stay long. Curtain's in less than two hours."

"Come in. Come in. Rupert, get the man's coat."

Splat Bobbins pushed the prop door to shut it. He reached for the shoes again. Then he realized the closing door had produced no sound. He reached over to finish closing the portal by hand. It would not close. That's when Abby Francis screamed.

On his feet in an instant George Chance could see why the door did not close. And why the woman screamed. When the door was opened a human arm had fallen through the opening. An arm with the hand covered in blood!

An hour and a half later, amid the bright lights of police flashbulbs, George Chance looked back on the moments after Abby Francis' scream. Almost instantly the lighted "On The Air" signs on all four walls of the studio went dark. Chance hurried towards the miniature door. As he passed the control room window he could see producer Herbert Johnston holding down a lever as he spoke into a microphone. A half decent lip-reader Chance made out the words "technical difficulties" as he passed.

Very carefully he gripped the wrist of the bloody arm. No pulse and the blood was dry. Pulling out a handkerchief to cover his fingers he swung the prop door open. To his surprise the door opened onto a small room. Dr. Robert Demarest, the city's Chief Medical Examiner, long ago had taught him how to check for a throat pulse. None there, either. Not surprising when he took note of the large knife embedded in the man's back.

Projecting his voice to make sure all heard him Chance announced, "This man is dead. Murdered. Control room, please call the police."

Some time later Ralph Owens voice came over the speaker from the control room, "The cops are entering the elevator 'cording to the guards."

Chance took a deep breath. Keeping this group of personalities away from the body made him think of herding cats. He glanced around. Behind the host's microphone he saw Herbert Johnston flipping through Lamar Richards' show folder. Then he froze for an instant. With an almost slight-of-hand motion Johnston slipped one sheet out of the folder. His hands below the tabletop, his arms moved as if he were wadding something up. A moment later his right hand slipped in and out of the pocket of his suit jacket. A moment later the cops, led by Detective Sergeant Ben Franklin Smith, entered the small broadcast complex.

As Johnston hastened forward to greet the law Chance pushed by him. He deftly removed a wadded paper from producer's pocket. He palmed the thing into a hidden pocket of his own jacket.

Finally back at home Chance slipped on thin cotton gloves to open up the paper. A bit of an unusual paper, he decided. The top of the paper contained a typewritten list marked "This Week's Plugs." One item had been scratched out with two additional things blue penciled in. The bottom of the page contained a mimeographed group of things to "Never Mention." Perplexed, the master magician put the paper aside.

Monday morning Chance decided to pop into Sardi's for a very early lunch. Joe Harper, his perpetual house guest, had more or less cleaned out his home 'Fridge again. Before he finished shaking hands with Vincent Sardi there came a call of "Hello Little George!" Sardi smiled broadly. He was one of the few who knew the story of that nickname for the six-foot-one magician.

A moment later George Chance shook hands once again with "Big George." That is "The Man Who Owns Broadway," George M. Cohan. As a lad, when his circus played New York, George was one of a dozen circus kids who performed in one of the great George M.'s reviews. After he instinctively answered to the call of "George!" a few times he officially became "Little George" for the remainder of the run. The two Georges had been friends for over twenty years.

As George Chance seated himself George M. remarked, "Saw you made the wrong kind of headlines last night, youngster."

"That I did, pal."

"Strange thing. I've been trying to get somebody on that show for a couple of months. *Return of the Vagabond* is about to open I'll take just about any publicity I can get.

"But where are my manners? George Chance, meet Celeste Holm, one of our featured players. She had a nice run in *The Time of Your Life*, you may remember."

Pleasantries concluded, George M. continued, "When it became clear *Who's In Town?* didn't want an old warhorse like me on, I tried to get Celeste booked as an up and coming actress. The show used to do that a lot before the sponsor changed hands. But that's water over the dam now. What else are you up to these days?"

After a pleasant lunch "Little" George Chance headed for Police Commissioner Standish's office. On the way he stopped at a pay phone to dial his own unlisted phone number.

On the third ring "Tinker to Evers to Chance," came out of the earpiece.

"Can the corn, Joe," Chance told Joe Harper, his permanent houseguest. "Get out of my easy chair and head over to the Wonderful Bakery." He gave the address. "That's just up Vinegar Hill from the Brooklyn Navy Yard. See if they're hiring. Your call about applying, or not. Then check out the neighborhood. Schmooze for anything that's happened since the place got bought out. Take the area's temperature. Got it?"

"Got it! New case?"

"I'm not sure yet. This is related to that murder last night. Wonderful is the radio show's sponsor. Oh, before you leave, ask Tim to get in touch with his librarian friend. See if she can find out exactly who bought Wonderful Bakery."

"That all, George?"

"That better not be all!" came an irate young woman's voice. "What you got for me, lover?"

Chance took a deep breath. He could just see Merry White's green eyes flashing at not being included. He thought fast. "All right Merry," he said, "Make up an identity as a new in town actress. Give her a fairly strong history of parts played. Type up her resume using five or six carbon copies. Dress up like an out-of-towner and then go down to the *Who's In Town?* studio in Rockefeller Center. Try to get booked on the show. Give them the last readable carbon copy of the resume, if they'll take it. Your character doesn't know about the murder. But, if there are police there, or something, get all wide eyed and ask what's going on. But, remember, this may all be for nothing."

"Oh, George, you really know how to make a girl feel... well... Ahh, Hades! It beats sitting around here all day!"

George Chance was still chuckling to himself as he hung up the phone.

"Dr. Demarest tells me the body was almost *not* discovered, George," said Police Commissioner Standish with a wry smile on his rocky jaw. "If he'd been killed half an hour sooner, maybe even less, rigor mortis would have kept the arm from moving. I doubt any of you would have seen it then."

"Not the *ghost* of a chance," replied Chance with a wink. "Anything more?"

"The good doctor also says, based on the blood marks in the photos of that 'prop room,' the man did not die immediately. He tried to crawl out through that door, but didn't make it."

"I'm going to have to get a look in that little room."

"Why am I not surprised? And not even a moral dilemma for me. The detectives working the case have already alibied you out of suspicion. Given the estimated time of death, your gaggle of students at the New York School of Magic told 'em that you never disappeared for more than a couple minutes at a time."

Standish rose and closed the office door. As he reseated himself he asked, "You going to take this on as a case?"

"Not sure yet, Commissioner. Something just doesn't sit right with me. Plus I just picked up one bit about the radio show that the detectives working the case may not see. You-know-who will take a quick look. If he decides not to pursue the matter I'll turn everything over to your fellows."

It is positively amazing, decided Joe Harper, *what information you can pry out of folks at a lunch counter. Provided you get there before the rush starts.*

Harold's Fast & Tasty on Vinegar Hill sported a dozen counter stools and a bunch of small tables that constantly got moved around. The marks on the freshly swept floor proved that. Joe sipped at his coffee as he began to munch on his second piece of fresh from the oven pie.

"Honey," said Shelley, one of the pair of waitresses, "we'll need that stool in about fifteen minutes. If ya cut it too close you'll be like a salmon swimming upstream just to get out the door."

"Gotcha, doll," replied Joe. "Appreciate the chance to sit down after walking the area all morning. My brother's started to drive here from Indy yesterday. Got to find a place for us to room. You know any places where we could have a private entrance? My brother sometimes works nights and weird hours."

"Honey, I know just the place. Abby, the widow Jenkins, that is, just had the attic fixed up to add more boarding space. You and your brother may have to duck a bit in spots, but the Fire Department made her put in an outside stair to it. Let me write down the address. Place's up by the Admiral's quarters."

Merry White headed for the Women's Room at the edge of the rotunda at Rockefeller Center. As always she felt a bit uncomfortable as the eyes of the characters on the painted ceilings seemed to follow her everywhere she went. Once inside she changed her lipstick to an even brighter shade. Then she widened her eye-shadow. Viewing the results in the mirror she grimaced a bit. But, the look went with the medium brunette wig she wore. With more wiggle in her walk than normal she headed for the elevators.

The building stood only a few blocks from George Chance's brownstone, but the neighborhood could not be more different. Next to a disused high twin-spire church, the boxy house once served as the church's Rectory. The place was said to be haunted. Above ground the house looked the part. The advertised rental price for the dwelling went past the far side of outrageous.

However, if you knew how to safely enter the door at the bottom of the back stairwell, the basement of the Rectory housed a workshop any master illusionist would covet. A scientific laboratory adjoined the workshop. But, this early evening's get together used the basement's living room. Or perhaps parlor would be the better term.

As they entered Merry White and Glennn Saunders tossed their oversized hats at a rack on the wall as they shed light, but long coats. They began cleaning up the parlor and the attached kitchen and dining area. Five minutes later Tiny Tim Terry entered. Using a tall bench he dusted and restocked the large bar.

By the time George Chance entered the place looked ready to be shown to a perspective tenant. "Is the food here?" he called out.

After a negative chorus of replies Chane stepped over to the bar to accept a bubbling Highball from Tim Terry. He managed only a few sips when Joe Harper staggered in with three large sacks of Chinese takeout.

By custom they ate without reference to current issues. Instead they recalled times past and people they had met while touring the United States and places beyond. Each read their cookie fortunes to hoots of laughter from the others. Then, libations at hand, things took a serious turn.

"The murdered man was Joseph Parkinson," began Chance. "His show name was Joe Parks or Parks'N'Rec. He actually worked for the City's Parks Department. He covered non-commercial outdoor activities. So far nobody remembers seeing him there the day of the murder. He played softball and managed a team in one of the local recreational leagues. Also a HAM radio operator. New York's Finest are putting his life and recent activities under a microscope. I'll get copies of their reports if we continue to pursue the case. Mary?"

"Gloria, the receptionist at the studio," continued Merry, "is part time. In fact she's the only behind the scenes employee, besides Splat, who worked there before Wonderful Bakery got bought out. She works 10:00 to 3:00 five days a week. She's never there any other time. When I asked about getting on the show she told me all sorts of things have changed with the "new" sponsor. And never with any explanation given.

"Beyond that, I got three very interesting bits of information from her. First, before the Wonderful buy out, somebody offered to buy the studio's lease for quite a bit of money. The old management turned the offer down. Too much trouble getting production space elsewhere, and on short notice. Not to mention the supposed boost the Rockefeller Center address gives the show. Second, after the buy out, she got two week's paid leave while the offices and studio got remodeled. Third, since the remodeling, a person, or persons, unknown spends quite a bit of time in the offices when she's not there. At least one of those visitors smokes Lucky-Strikes like a chimney.

"After that I headed to the Daily Star. I sweet-talked Robb, the Morgue manager, into getting me a list of everybody who's been on the show for the last year. That should be ready tomorrow."

Tim Terry reported next, "Wonderful Bakery, Inc. was a closely held family run corporation. Other than family members, only a few long time employees owned stock. Just enough stockholders that the details of the sale had to be reported to the Securities Commission. The selling price ended up being nearly fifty percent above the estimated value of the company. Jean, my librarian friend, found that the money was paid to the stockholders by some sort of front company called Alliance Partners. The company's address is the office of a lawyer who specializes in that sort of thing. Jean'll let me know if she's able to find out anything about Alliance's backers. She's not too optimistic."

"Things are a bit tense on Vinegar Hill," began Joe Harper. "But the situation at Wonderful is only a small part of it. Ever since the war drums started pounding in Europe, there's been all sorts of speculation about the Brooklyn Navy Yard. During the last war they expanded the Yard big time. Some folks are afraid half, or maybe all, of Vinegar Hill could get annexed. The Wonderful plant on the Hill has been running at near capacity for years. About eighteen months ago, before it changed hands, the company bought land in Jersey to build a second bakery. A bigger one. Good planning, to my way of thinking, 'cause the old plant would probably be included in any version of the Navy Yard expanding.

"I asked about a job at the bakery. The acting Personnel Manager told me his boss just quit 'cause the new management's doing the hiring direct and not from the neighborhood. Guys show up with letters of introduction that include exactly what positions they'll be assigned to. A lot of the old employees are getting bussed to Jersey to get the new plant up and running. I got the notion that the acting guy's about ready to jump ship, too.

"I spent a little time at the favorite bar of the union bakers. Seems the new guys join the union, but don't want participate in any after hours stuff. They show up on time, do what they're supposed to, and that's it. But they got no pride in their work. Not particularly friendly at work, either. Seems downright squirrely."

"Thanks, friends," said George Chance. "Please keep quietly digging. Joe, did you happen to rent a room on Vinegar Hill?"

"You bet, George! Comes with a private entrance and an attractive widowed landlady. Place is not that far from both the bakery and even closer to the Admiral's mansion, what they call Quarters A. My phony brother is supposed to get to town in the next day or two."

"Good. Get yourself settled in. Case the entire area. I may join you at any time. It all depends on what our friend finds out tonight."

In mid-June dusk seemed to take forever to fall. George Chance sat at his makeup table in the Rectory to bring "our friend" to life. First came the wire appliances. They changed the profile of his nose and elongated the nostrils. A fast drying brown concoction, applied with a brush, then darkened those nostrils. Also brown, eye-shadow gave his eyes a really sunken look. Highlighting made his cheekbones seem much higher and wider than the ones nature gave him.

He moved the mirror's wings until he could see all sides of his face. Satisfied, he began working an extremely dark brown jell into his golden locks. Soon he wore an almost black skullcap of patent-leather-hair.

Smoother than Chandu's, he thought to himself.

Then he began powdering his nose, not to mention all his exposed skin, including his hands. He ended up with the pallid completion of a mushroom. Satisfied with the skin he glued a set of over-dentures in place. The teeth looked like they had been fashioned from centuries old piano keys.

Chance worked a set of buttons on the makeup table. The mirror's array of light bulbs and the overhead fixtures went out. Only two small wall sconces remained lit. Pulling off the barber style sheet that protected his dark green suit, he adjusted his even darker green tie, then flipped a tiny switch behind it. The tie's tack style holder looked like a pearl older than the denture's teeth. But now a tiny bulb inside came to life to throw eerie green dim light and shadows on his face.

Then George Chance tested what he called *Putting on the Ghost.* His well trained facial muscles pulled his lips away from the tarnished ivory teeth. His eyes seemed to glaze over, as if seeing nothing. His entire head now resembled more a bare skull than a living human being.

He let his face relax. Now he simply looked like an unfortunate human who did not get enough sun. He chuckled a bit. Donning a slouch hat that exactly matched his suit, the Green Ghost went on the hunt.

The ding of the floor's elevator bell brought the Police Officer out of the chair between the doors of the *Who's In Town?* studio and offices. He had not been dozing, but that was not for lack of temptation. All traffic on floor had ended hours ago when the uniformed custodian departed. He wondered if he would even see who just arrived. Chances seemed to favor the visitor going to a business in another wing.

Then a man strode purposefully around the corner. The Officer looked over his shoulder to be sure he was not being diverted from someone arriving via the stairs. Then he took a close look at his visitor. The good sized man wore the darkest green suit the cop could remember seeing.

…he could see all sides of his face.

And, the big slouch hat matched.

"Can I help you, sir?"

"Good evening, Officer. I am Gerald Orbach. I consult for Commissioner Standish. I have my introductory credentials right here," replied George Chance as he held up a passport like folder with stamps and a picture of the face he wore embossed with the department's official seal. He handed the document over, then stepped back out of reach. The Gerald Orbach disguise was one he had often used in the past when working with the police. "What's your name, Officer?"

"Burland, sir," replied the cop as he glanced at the paperwork. He took another look over his shoulder. Then he gave the folder his full attention.

"You're a cautious man, Burland. I like that."

"Thank you, Mr. Orbach. Maybe I read too many issues of *Detective Fiction Weekly* for my own good. But..."

"...as Molly Goldberg says, on the radio, 'Couldn't hurt.'" finished Chance. "I need to get a look inside. You have the keys?"

About midnight Joe Harper slipped out the attic door of the widow Jenkins' rooming house. He'd made a point of bringing in his belongings up that way. He now knew how to avoid all the creaks of the new wooden stairs. In a black sports shirt and pants, plus a black fedora, he blended well with the night.

Without appearing furtive he quietly strolled to the Admiral's house. Commanders of the Brooklyn Navy Yard had billeted at the mansion for well over a century. As he walked by the gate he waved at the uniformed Marine on duty. He continued for two blocks, then circled back towards the Wonderful Bakery. To his surprise, there seemed to be some activity there.

Three of the company's medium sized delivery trucks were backed up to loading doors. Joe ducked into the two foot space between the buildings across the street. Out of his pocket came a large black handkerchief. He tied the cloth just below his eyes and pulled his fedora even lower. Virtually invisible, he watched.

No lights showed. He heard nothing but night noises. Then the back end of one of the trucks dipped as if a man had stepped aboard carrying something fairly heavy. Over the next five minutes each of the trucks moved in the same way more than once.

Then a bit of light glowed for a brief moment in the cab of one truck. The dash lights, thought Joe. A moment later the truck quietly started, but no lights came on. Slowly, almost silently, the truck pulled forward to the street and turned downhill in the direction of the Navy Yard. Joe saw the vehicle turn right three blocks down. A moment later the process began again with the second truck.

Joe sprinted back along the niche between the buildings. All the while he prayed he wouldn't smash into some fence or wall. He burst onto the next street over to turn hard left on the downslope. His crape soled shoes made little noise. Just before the third intersection he managed to stop with the help of a large mailbox.

He looked to the right. No sign of the first truck. Crouching behind the mailbox he waited, hoping the second truck followed the first. It did. Lights still off the vehicle silently rolled by. The streetlight showed him, just barely, that two men rode in the cab. Two blocks past the mailbox the truck turned left.

Again Joe sprinted; this time down the sidewalk. There was just enough light to keep him from crashing into things. At the second turn he ducked behind a small shuttered newsstand. Near the bottom of the hill he saw the second truck backing up to the right.

He almost dashed across the street, but something held him back. Well he did, for as the third truck approached, it slowed into the turn. As it did a man stepped out of a vestibule on the side street. He jumped to the cab's small running-board and grabbed the mirror and door handle for balance.

Joe felt his knees shake a bit. He'd nearly plunged right by the lookout. He stayed behind the newsstand. Less than twenty minutes later the parade of blacked out trucks reversed itself in the direction of the bakery. But this time the trucks seemed loaded much more heavily. Heart still pounding a bit, Joe Harper crept back to the widow Jenkins' place.

In Manhattan George Chance sat cross legged on the gravel roof of a rare one story building below Canal Street. Looking just over the place's false front, he watched the light and shadows in the second floor of the building across the street. As he waited for the office of the lawyer fronting for Alliance Partners to go dark, he went back over his time at the *Who's In Town?* offices and studio.

"Sir," said Officer Burland as he opened the studio door, "should you want to take anything with you, I'll have to fill out an inventory slip for you to sign."

George pulled a small Lica camera out of his pants' pocket. "I imagine I can make do with this," he replied as they went up the three steps to the control room floor. He knew that radio and sound studios were almost always raised above the base floor to facilitate running all the cables necessary for production. Normally the area under the control board could be popped open for troubleshooting. In this case the pedestal appeared completely sealed.

In the studio proper the other ends of the cables came out of boxes blind bolted into the floor. He looked around, but could see nothing new to him. He walked over to Splat's sound effect area. He gave it a good look because he didn't want Officer Burland thinking he'd been there before. Finally he opened the prop door.

He closed the door as he'd seen Splat try to do. The small room behind the miniature portal caused a slight echo when the door slammed. Re-opening the door he crawled inside the prop room. He flipped the light switch on the inside jamb. The room seemed to be about three-and-a-half feet deep and six or seven feet wide. Some spare microphones and cables hung on the long walls. Sound effect gimcracks were everywhere. He studied the bloodstains on the floor. He also noticed traces of fingerprint powder in various places. He stepped to the far end of the tiny room. Nothing hung on this wall, but boxes of Splat's stock-in-trade sat on the floor. Using a handkerchief he moved one of the boxes to see how the wall joined the floor. Then he looked at the construction of the wall corners and ceiling.

Officer Burland, leaning in thru the prop door could not see the grim smile that flickered across the Green Ghost's face.

Soon they surveyed the office part of the radio program's operation. Chance paid extra attention to the decor of the remodeled offices. Of particular interest was the large closet in the executive office. In it the lingering smell of cigarettes could be cut with a knife. Chance thanked Officer Burland and quietly headed for the Center's roof. He picked a lock to get outside. After a brief search he took two flash pictures of the *Who's In Town?*'s relay antenna that sent the program to the Lamont network. Then he departed for the shell company office.

Now, on the single story roof, Chance pulled out his pocket watch and opened it. The timepiece had no crystal. He read the time with his rubber cement coated fingertips as the blind do. Almost midnight. Less than five minutes later the lights across the street finally went out. Five minutes after that he listened at the door of the lawyer's suite.

He had just inserted his picks into the door lock when he heard sounds in the nearby stairwell. Chance yanked out the picks. A short moment later he closed the door of a janitor's closet behind him. Turning he opened the door just a crack. A few seconds later a man hurried past him. The fellow wore a snappy black business suit with a gray fedora and slightly rundown shoes. Quickly, he opened the front company's door and slammed it behind him.

Chance stuck his head out of the closet. He just barely heard a voice say, "Operator, get me..." But the man lowered his excited voice as he gave the number. *Well, my name isn't Chance for nothing,* Chance mused as he stepped back to the fateful door. He listened carefully to one side of the phone call.

"Daily here... Yeah, we got lucky. Graver found me two blocks over having a sandwich. You got something for me? Heath!?! He's still making trouble? Okay, got any idea where he'll be? The Blue Rose? Yeah, I know it. If he stays 'til closing, I can be there in plenty of time. Fine, but you can pay for that sandwich I didn't finish... Ha! Call it petty cash... I'd better get moving..."

With that the Green Ghost's dark green crape soled shoes made hasty, but silent tracks for the stairs.

George Chance watched the street from the darkened vestibule of a tailor shop on the building's ground floor. During the short wait he rattled his memory for something called the Blue Rose. No luck. Then his quarry emerged from the building's lobby.

Daily walked to the bus stop on the block. He looked at the posted schedule, then shook his head. Chance ducked to the back of the vestibule, nearly invisible, as Daily purposely hurried by. *Headed for the subway,* Chance decided. He followed at a distance the two blocks. As soon as his quarry turned for the subway stairs Chance caught up as much as he safely could.

Special pockets sewn into his clothing held both change and every possible transportation token he might need. He actually passed Daily as the man scanned the schedule listings. As soon as he indicated the set of turnstiles he intended to use Chance entered ahead of him. Now they waited on the platform with a small handful of others. Chance kept most of the other people between himself and Daily. When the train rolled up, he entered the car behind his man.

Daily seemed a little nervous. Instead of sitting in the nearly empty car, Chance watched him strap-hang through the windows in the doors between the rail cars. He continued to follow Daily through one change of trains. Finally the man got off at a stop near Vinegar Hill.

Daily hurried out of the station. Chance came as close behind the man as he dared. For a moment he feared he'd lost his quarry. Then he saw Daily cross the almost deserted street ahead. Chance stayed on the opposite side and hurried along. Daily turned left to head up the hill. Taking advantage of the little cover available, Chance managed to be out of sight the couple of times Daily looked behind himself.

Then, about three blocks up the hill, Chance saw a small mostly blue neon sign. Pulling a pair of opera glasses from a pocket, he soon discovered that he and Daily approached the Blue Rose Bar and Grill.

At the next intersection Chance turned right. As soon as he lost sight of Daily he bolted around the next corner and sprinted up the hill. When Daily took up a position to watch the door of the Blue Rose, Chance already held down a position to watch *him*. Then both men waited.

About one o'clock men, and an occasional woman began to drift out of the bar. Tomorrow was a workday, after all. Daily watched intently, but did not move.

Almost thirty minutes later two men stepped outside. They shook hands, then headed in opposite directions. Daily followed the younger man heading up hill from the other side of the street. Chance ducked into an alley. He crouched behind some trash cans let this fellow Heath get ahead of him. The man wore laborer's clothes with what Chance thought might be a union patch at the top of his right sleeve.

As they neared the top of Vinegar Hill, Heath turned toward the East River and the quarters of the Commandant of the Navy Yard. For some reason this made Daily close in.

The man moved silently as he crossed the street to come up behind Heath. Something in each of his hands glinted in the dim glow of a lamppost. Still on the sidewalk down the hill a bit from the cross street, Chance ran for all he was worth. As Daily came even with the curb, Chance bounded to the trunk, then roof of a car parked at the corner. Daily heard the sound of bending sheet metal. He spun to his right as the Green Ghost flung himself from the hood of the car right at him.

Daily took a step-and-a-half back on pure reflex. The Green Ghost executed a perfect aerial summersault to land on his feet, knife in hand. Daily's mouth dropped open, but he charged at the interloper.

The Green Ghost took in his adversary in a tiny splinter of time. Daily held a shiny leather covered blackjack in his right hand. In his left was a long switchblade. The Green Ghost stepped aside with astonishing speed, pivoting to his right as he did so. Daily could not move his knife hand far or fast enough to strike anything as he thundered by.

The Green Ghost's left hand slammed into Daily's shoulder with explosive force. Daily sidestepped to keep from falling. Then the bumper of the parked car brought his legs to an instant halt. Daily sprawled across the hood. His arms then explosively shoved him off of the car. He landed upright on the street ready to fight.

The Green Ghost readied himself. Then behind him came the strident shrill of a Boatswain's pipe in a two note call. Daily moved forward deliberately, knife now in his right hand, his face confident.

The Ghost kept his knife hand at the ready position. But his left arm jerked and moved. Something dropped out of his sleeve into the firm grasp of his last two fingers. Then his thumb and forefinger threw the switch behind his tie.

Daily kept his eyes on the almost unmoving face of his opponent. People usually led with their faces. Then the face somehow became lit up. The man's eyes seemed empty, like the victims in that movie, *White Zombie.* Now the man's lips drew away from his teeth. They seemed to disappear entirely. Suddenly Daily gazed on the face of *Death* itself.

He froze. The Green Ghost smashed the sphere in his left hand to the ground in front of the man while he closed his eyes.

An orange flash blinded Daily. Then a rising cloud of smoke enveloped his face. His eyes instantly watered. That's when the Green Ghost stepped forward to prick Daily's wrist to loosen the knife, then deliver a smashing backhand blow to the head. Daily folded like an old leather wallet.

The Green Ghost heard feet pounding on the pavement behind him. He turned to see a blinking Heath fumbling for a gun in an ankle holster. From up the street a pair of Marines ran fill tilt with Colt Model 1911 automatics at the ready. Since he did not want to simply disappear, the Green Ghost dug out his police credentials.

Rear Admiral Clark H. Woodward looked at the unusual man seated at the other end of the dining room table in his quarters. He used the room for small and discrete meetings. *Strange man, stranger results*, he thought. Present when the Sergeant of the Guard threw a bucket of cold water on the would be assassin, the fellow sputtered back to consciousness moaning about having seen the face of death.

"Mr. Orbach," he said as he placed the telephone receiver in the cradle, "the Watch Commander at Police Headquarters has vouched for you. He seemed a little startled to have to do so."

"That's not surprising, sir. I report directly to the Commissioner. Chances are I've never laid eyes on tonight's Officer of the Watch. He just followed what's in his Standard Operating Procedures."

"Don't we all," chuckled the Admiral. "Now, please tell me how you ended up giving us some big help tonight."

"Working a seemingly unrelated case I happened to hear this Daily get his orders. Sounded like 'Dirty Work at the Crossroads' so I tagged along. May I ask what type of mission Heath is working on?"

"Boatswain's Mate Heath is a very promising young Petty-Officer. He grew up on Vinegar Hill. He joined the Navy after moving to California. One of my Staff Officers served with him. No one on the Atlantic coast knows he's Navy. We brought him in to track down some very strange stories being told about this area. An old family friend hired him to run some Union errands. Until tonight nothing he's found out seemed threatening at all, just weird."

"Weird is one thing I keep an eye out for, Admiral. By the way, I take it your opinion of the international situation has not changed since you were quoted in the New York Sun."

"While improvements are happening," said the Admiral, "we still can't protect both our coasts. Even more today, the future it looks as if we will have enemies in both the Atlantic and the Pacific. That's why I brought Heath in when ghost stories about the area began to circulate. We can't afford to take any chances."

"We're going to put this Daily in the brig of a ship bound for Baltimore. He'll quietly be charged with interfering with an investigation. Our people out of D.C. will find out what he knows. Now, if you should come across anything more *we* should know, or need help, here is the number for the Yard's Staff Duty Officer. This slip of paper contains the challenges and passwords for the next week. Please memorize and destroy it before you leave.

"By the way, I'll pass my personal thanks on to Commissioner Standish when I see him on Thursday."

"Thank you, sir. Where will that be?"

"The weekly Civil Defense Committee meeting at Rockefeller Center."

George Chance got a few hours sleep on the couch at the Rectory. Just after dawn on Tuesday he called a meeting with his team. By the time they all arrived a twelve egg omelet filled a covered platter as Chance flipped flapjacks on the range's built in grill.

"I may have a full day ahead of me," said Chance around a mouthful, "so let's get straight to reports. Merry…"

"Robb got me the list of show guests. We talked about it for nearly half-an-hour. A couple of things stood out. First, almost nobody from Europe's been on. Absolutely nobody from England, that's sure. In general, guests known to be against getting involved in any war in Europe sure outnumber those for it. That fellow you met, Arthur Raymond, he's the third guy booked from that small production of 'All Quiet on the Western Front.' Make what you want out of that, Lover."

"Somethin' definitely weird at Wonderful Bakery," continued Joe.

Nobody spoke as Joe concluded. They knew their boss's mind would be racing like Barney Oldfield at Indianapolis. A few moments later George Chance looked down at an empty plate. He did not remember eating more than three bites.

"Somebody connected to the front company got told to kill or capture, kill, more likely, a guy doing union organizing on Vinegar Hill," Chance said finally. "Turns out he's undercover for the Navy. This is getting more complicated by the minute.

"Merry, you still have that press card for that chain of local advertising papers? Good. You head over to Wonderful's new bakery in Jersey. Talk to the management about bringing jobs to the area. Also try to talk to some of the workers getting bussed in. See what they're thinking. Keep your eyes open for anything that doesn't seem to fit in. But, before that, get this roll of film developed. Take the prints of the radio antenna over to Hugo Gernsback's office. Ask if there's anything strange or unusual about them. If he can't help you, he'll know who can.

"Joe, you scout the area where those trucks went. Come up with a good reason to be there. We don't want you making waves. Tim, keep

Chance...called a meeting of his team...

looking into the front company. While you're at it, call the Rockefeller Center offices. See if they have a list of meetings and activities available. Get chatty. See how loose lipped they are. Glennn, I need you to cover that charity show I have this afternoon.

"I'm going to talk to Standish, then head back to Rockefeller Center. If you don't hear from me we'll have breakfast again tomorrow."

Police Commissioner Standish found a man snoozing on his office couch when he arrived for an early meeting. Even with the fedora over the stranger's face, the dark green suit told him what he needed to know.

"I attend quite a number of meetings at Rockefeller Center," said Standish a couple of minutes later. "The management makes their rooms available to government agencies at little or no cost. They make up for it by charging fifteen cents per cup of coffee served. Multiple agencies can have meetings on neutral ground that way. The Civil Defense Committee meets every other Thursday in their biggest room. The Mayor is the chairman."

"Would you have your secretary quietly request a copy of the 'as built' plans for Rockefeller Center from the City Architect's office, along with copies of any building permits issued to modify the place since it opened? Oh, almost forgot, please add a set of maps for the Brooklyn Navy Yard and Vinegar Hill area." With that the Green Ghost headed for Vinegar Hill.

In a stall of a subway rest room George Chance popped out his yellowed over-dentures and slipped on a dark brown toupee. His dark green suit coat reversed to become a black sports jacket. Looking quite a bit different he climbed the stairs to the streets of the Vinegar Hill area.

He walked along the Navy Yard parameter to get the feel of the place. Then he began a round about exploration of the area Joe Harper reported on at breakfast. Some time later he almost fell over as he tried to contain gales of laughter.

Joe Harper lived in George Chance's guest bedroom because there was very little hard work in the things Chance asked him to do in an unspoken contract for the privilege. Danger Joe could handle, hard work, not so much. Now he found Joe, stripped down to his undershirt, handkerchief serving as a sweatband, swinging a pick and shovel in the small front yard of a very old house.

Still laughing inwardly, Chance retraced his steps to a tiny market a block over. There he bought two twelve ounce bottles of Pepsi-Cola out of a tub of ice. Returning, he walked up behind Joe.

"Your brother's here," he said quietly. Joe picked up the cue as if they'd rehearsed for hours.

"Willie, you made it! Glad to see you. Come on, this way. There's shade on the steps." Anyone passing by would have heard him. "Been making the rounds looking for odd jobs. Found an information mine here." Nobody but Chance heard that.

Chance had not opened the bottles of soda-pop. He knew Joe always carried an opener, but the device usually opened beer. They sat drinking, making small talk about Chance's supposed drive from Indianapolis. Then Joe dropped his voice.

"Mrs. Hutchinson's family's lived here for over a hundred years. She gave me the scoop on where those trucks went. The place is called the Robbins mansion. See, between the two houses across the street, that old house. Back when, her family worked for the owners; big shots that owned horses. Can't see them from here, but there are big stables and what used to be a portico to the house itself. The last son of the family converted the stables to an automobile repair shop. Then, during the Great War, the guy landed a subcontract with the Navy Yard and enclosed the portico for more work space.

"About six years ago the man and his whole family were found butchered in a barricaded room on the top floor. Cops had to cut through a wall to get in."

"I remember that," exclaimed George Chance. "The Robbins Murders. We were playing Fargo, North Dakota, at the time, but the crime still got a lot of ink in the local paper. It was never solved, as I remember."

"Correct. The place's been sealed ever since. Nobody's been able to locate the heir who'd been a medical missionary in Mongolia when last heard from. For the last few years, even before Wonderful Bakery grew to such a regional powerhouse, weird things have been going on around that place. Haunted sorts of things. Everybody in the neighborhood keeps their distance."

"Whew," whistled Chance, "there's another wing-of-bat, or eye-of-newt, to add to this strange caldron. But how did you end up digging for China?"

"Mrs. Hutchinson planted a new flowerbed this spring. Everything turned up their noses and died. In exchange for a hot lunch and gossip, I agreed to turn the soil over much deeper than she could. We chatted while she sat out on these steps snapping beans and peeling spuds while I dug. Then I discovered there's a hundred plus year old rain cistern right under most of the garden area. She's got me finding the edges so she can figure out what to do next."

Back at Commissioner Standish's office Chance found a several heavy rolls of plans waiting for him, along with some smaller loose papers. The whole pile stank of the ammonia based copying developer. Tying his suit-coat around the whole mess, he staggered out of the building. The cab driver complained of the stench when he dropped Chance off near the Rectory.

In the building's basement he unfolded the legs of several card tables to receive the rolled papers. Eyes watering at times, he began a close examination of the plans for the studio's floor and any changes to it. Tiny Tim Terry wandered in a couple of hours later. Soon cigar smoke competed with the ammonia fumes in the basement.

"Jean, my librarian friend, had some luck," Tim reported. "In one of the now out-of-date business directories she found that some of the same people associated with the Wonderful Bakery buy out are also 'angels' for the "All Quiet on the Western Front" production. Then she traced some of the other names from the production to Alliance Partners and another group that seems to be throwing money at any activity that leans toward isolation from the rest of the world. Sounds to me like their bread might be getting buttered by the Fascists. I really hope that's not the case!"

"So do I," agreed Chance, "but, we'd better operate as if they are. Sure fits in with that murder attempt. After everybody else reports in, I'm going back to Rockefeller Center. In the meantime, slip out and call to see if Gio's small back room is available. Have everybody meet there. I'll be darned if I'm going to eat here until these fumes are gone."

Later, at Gio's excellent Italian restaurant, Chance spoke as he sectioned a pan of lasagna while Tim poured Chianti. "Assuming the worst for the backers of Alliance Partners, they could be planning to sabotage both the

Brooklyn Navy Yard and Rockefeller Center. Merry, what did you find out today?"

"Mr. Gernsbeck sent me to see a fellow named Burgess over at Westinghouse Laboratories. The guy was helpful, but he seemed more interested in getting my phone number. Just so you know, lover!"

"From the pictures by themselves he didn't see anything unusual. Then I told him that it served as a feed to a network. Now that lit him up. He said the antenna looked like a standard general broadcast one. Meaning the signal is meant to go in all directions. But, to feed a network, he'd expect to see a whole different kind of setup. One where all of the broadcast power would be channeled in the direction of the network's pickup antenna.

"Then he waved an issue of that *Agent 9* pulp magazine at me. Said that this writer, Chuck Kennedy, used something called a subcarrier as the issue's weird plot device. On the subcarrier you could send messages that nobody could hear unless they had a special receiving set. That if you used a wire-recorder, or maybe a Dict-A-Phone you could speed up either Morse code or voices so that nobody listening in could understand anything. Doesn't that sound creepy?"

"My doing work for Mrs. Hutchinson paid off," reported Joe. "Neighbors who saw me digging acted like they already knew me. I talked to as many as I could. It boils down to this. All kinds of strange noises, but mostly not really loud ones, are coming from the Robbins Mansion itself, and the shops. And the street lights anywhere near the property are always out. The city puts in new bulbs, or even new fixtures, they're busted again in three days, tops. Nobody ever sees it happen. A couple of people have heard what might be those trucks, but haven't been able to see enough to be sure for the darkness."

After midnight the Green Ghost returned to Rockefeller Center. He rode the elevator two floors higher than the studio. Taking the stairs furthest from the studio he quietly emerged on the proper floor. Soon he stood in front of a door marked Apex Consultants. He carried a stethoscope and he applied the cone to the door as he listened closely. He also listened to places along the wall in both directions but heard nothing. After several minutes he picked the lock.

Apex Consultants' waiting room looked like any other. However, everywhere but the receptionist's desk needed dusting except for where the morning's edition of the New York Comet lay. Nobody appeared to have so much as looked at the thing.

The door leading to the work area sported an expensive Yale deadbolt lock. Again the Ghost listened at the door and the walls with the same results; nothing. Then he spent a sweaty five minutes defeating the lock without leaving a mark.

The two offices immediately behind the door looked normal and regularly used. Each had a Dict-A-Phone. To the right was a very large supply room. The place contained a huge stock of pencils, stenographer's paper notebooks, plus a half dozen typewriters set up for transcription, and shelf after shelf of canned food.

The door to the left of the offices also sported a Yale lock. George entered and flipped on the light. For a second he thought he'd been transported to the Wild West, for the place resembled the bunkhouse of a ranch. Double high bunks hugged three of the walls. A hotplate and kitchen utensils littered a table attached to the fourth wall. Another table, near the room's center, held cards, books and magazines, plus overflowing ashtrays.

Across from where the Ghost stood was something that should not have been there; a door. Three heavy bolts kept the portal from so much as rattling. He eased them back, then opened it. As he had suspected from the modified building plans, he found himself in the executive closet of the *Who's In Town?* studio.

Out in the studio's office lobby he again examined the walls enclosing the murder room. Art Deco brass trim about three inches wide enveloped the wall's right angle turn. About chest high he spotted some smudged fingerprints on the brass work. A minute later he felt something click under his probing fingers. He pulled and the end wall of the prop room swung open. He smiled as he saw blind hinges very similar to ones he used to make some of his stage illusions work.

Now he understood the murder. The "how" part, anyway. Joe Parks got stabbed in the back in the reception area. Before he could fall the killer opened the secret door to shove him into the prop room. But why? Then the Green Ghost noticed that the area under the raised floor of the prop room was wide open.

The Green Ghost spent the next three hours crawling through the guts of Rockefeller Center. Just before four A.M. he withdrew the way he came erasing, he hoped, all traces of his visit.

Wednesday morning found a blurry eyed George Chance talking to his team.

"You won't believe what I found inside Rockefeller Center. The studio's control room butts up against an air shaft. Unlike the areas that carry electricity, water and phone lines, nobody even looks in these shafts except when there's trouble. But, in case of trouble, they're set up so men can move around in them. With a little extra gear and a few hidden doors I got to every significant area of the whole building. Somebody has very quietly put in a bunch of 'improvements' to the system.

"I got the dope on pretty much the whole system. Today we're going to design and build some surprises..."

Wednesday evening, after dinner, Admiral Woodward entered his private study to find the light on his desk already on and the overhead fixture out of action. He took a step forward when an echoing voice froze him in place.

"Good evening, Admiral."

"What? Who... How did you get in here?" His chest swelled with a deep breath.

"No need to yell, Admiral. I'm here to help you. Look, I am standing by your wonderful old globe."

The eerie voice seemed to emanate from the entire room. Woodward turned toward the four foot diameter world globe in a low stand in the shadowed corner of the room. As his eyes adjusted he thought he could see a figure standing there. Just barely. Then an even eerier green glow illuminated the figure's head. He bit his tongue to keep from yelling as an animated skull peered back at him.

"Do you know who I am?"

Again the words seemed to bounce around the room. In spite of himself the Admiral shivered.

"According to my Intelligence staff some call you the Ghost or the Green Ghost. Your activities appear to be sanctioned by the NYPD. No wonder that attacker babbled about seeing Death's own face when he woke up. I assume this is no social call."

"You assume correctly, sir. There is a cloud of mystery that swirls around the new owners of the Wonderful Bakery that sits not far from here. Tendrils of that mystery appear to come even closer to the Navy Yard than the Bakery and extend into Manhattan, as well. Here is what I propose..."

Errand completed the Green Ghost drove his nondescript sedan to a loading dock about a block away from Rockefeller Center. He parked next to a panel truck with decals for a well known plumbing company. A moment later he climbed into the passenger seat of the truck. In a coverall, the driver sported a walrus mustache. Before he could settle himself in the driver yanked him over to plant a passionate kiss on his lips.

"Merry, what???" he sputtered.

"You tell your girl she's got to scrub off all her makeup, perfume and anything that smells like a woman. You do that and you can darn well kiss this soup strainer, lover. Now, let's get this show on the road," she concluded as her foot mashed the vehicle's starter. Even over the engine sounds George Chance could hear laughter from the rear of the truck.

A few moments later Officer Burland opened an almost hidden door at Rockefeller Center. Merry expertly backed the rear of the truck up to it. As she and a disguised Glenn Saunders began unloading tool boxes and materials the Green Ghost spoke to the young policeman.

"Thanks, Burland. You are officially relieved of duty for tonight. This envelope contains your instructions for tomorrow. You'll be undercover here in the Center. I've arranged delivery of what you'll need to your home this evening. Speak to absolutely no one about this. Understood?"

"You bet, sir! Glad to help out."

As soon as Burland departed Tiny Tim Terry emerged from a large box in the panel truck.

"Glad that part's over," he declared. "Let's get to work."

They did.

Abby Jenkins opened the door of her boarding house to find a familiar face smiling back at her.

"Randy Heath, as I live and breathe," she exclaimed as she reached up to hug the young man who once played with her children. "I heard you were back. Come in. Wonderful to see you."

"Great to see you, too, Mrs. Jenkins. I'm looking for one of your new borders, name of Joe Preston. Uncle Mike might have some work for him."

"I'm sure you remember how to get to the attic, Randy. He should be up there napping off dinner."

Joe Harper, currently going under the name Preston, opened the door to the stairs. He found a somber faced young man wearing very neat work clothing. The two exchanged a couple of cryptic phrases in low tones. Then Joe said, in a normal voice, "Work? Well, I'm not too fond of it, but come in and give me the low down."

With the door closed, he added, "Glad you made it. I hear my boss met with your boss."

"One of the housemen told me the Admiral looked white as a sheet after that meeting. That really surprised me. Woodward's a land combat veteran. That's about as tough as Navy officers come."

"You don't really know my boss," replied Joe with a smile. "You familiar with the Robbins place?"

"Sure, all the kids around here played with the Robbins boys. Used to run all over the front and back yards. That was ten years before the murders."

"Any haunted house stories about the place back then?" asked Joe.

"Nope, but there were a lotta weird noises. Years later I figured out that the sounds came from the huge old rain cistern. The thing was under most of the portico. When they converted the stables to cars, Mr. Robbins sold the last few horses, then dumped all the feed, manure and straw into the thing and sealed it off. Gasses used to whistle out of a couple of old capped off pipes in a thicket near the back line. One day a friend of mine lit a cigarette out there and got his eyebrows singed off. Darn lucky it wasn't worse."

"Come take a look at these maps," said Joe. "We got a couple of theories about what's going on. The place seems haunted these days, but we figure on Bundists, instead of ghosts."

Two hours later they had a plan to put before the authorities.

Glenn Saunders met George Chance at the Rectory at six o'clock on Thursday morning. At the same time Tiny Tim Terry slept fitfully in a section of an air vent a normal sized man could not enter. Each time he woke he cursed the fact that he had no cigars with him. *When this is over,* he promised himself, *I'm going to charge a box of ten cent cigars to petty cash!*

Glenn followed chance's instructions as he sat at the lighted makeup table. Finished, he donned a light brown wig followed by a light colored suit. He left the Rectory carrying a large gym bag. Three blocks over he hailed a passing cab. A few minutes later George Chance, in the guise of the Green Ghost, followed him.

The Green Ghost parked his car three blocks from Rockefeller Center. From a phone booth in an all-night drug store he called Commissioner Standish.

"Detective Smith found a radio of the type you mentioned in Parkinson's basement," reported the Commissioner. "One of our best radio techs is in the tower of the Chrysler Building using it to monitor transmissions. I've got a team of men at the precinct nearest the Manhattan location. They're ready to take off like those famous London Flying Squads."

At about the same time Joe Harper and Boatswains Mate Heath slipped in a nearly hidden gate to Quarters A at the corner of Evans and Little Streets. One of the uniformed Marines on duty there led them through the darkness and down a flight of stone stairs to the cellar.

The place seemed darker than outside. After a moment Joe realized that a number of men stood silently in an area off to his left. To his right he saw light leaking around a door at the head of a flight of wooden stairs leading to the first floor.

Seconds later that door opened. Light flooded down. Now Joe could see that over two dozen tough looking men in rough civilian clothes stood waiting in rows. Admiral Woodward and two other men in uniform descended to the cellar floor. The waiting men snapped to attention.

"As you were," said the Admiral. "Stand easy men. You are here today, in civies, because we believe that enemies of our country may be preparing sabotage against the Yard. As most of you know, the Posse Comitatus Act prevents the Navy from taking direct action against civilians. The same is not true about our sister service, the Coast Guard. That is why Commander Dawson and Chief Petty Officer Fournier are with us today..."

Joe Harper enjoyed the deception he and Heath, the young Navy man, perpetrated that morning. The two laughingly pushed a huge rectangular tub on wheels in the general direction of the Robbins mansion. As they moved along they drank frequently from Black Label beer bottles. Joe's one regret was that the bottles now held ginger ale. They told all they happened to meet that five cases of ice cold beer served to pay off a bet on last night's Brooklyn Dodgers game. Friends would be joining them soon. Every so often they added more empty bottles to the wire rack under the tub itself.

"We better wait for the others, before we have another," Heath told Joe as they pushed the tub under the shade of a tree in an empty lot that shared the back property line of the mansion.

Five burly men drifted up to the tub one by one. Dressed for work, each had a large Brooklyn Dodgers pin affixed to their hats or suspenders. They grew loud as they celebrated "th' Bums" nine to nothing shellacking of the St. Louis Cardinals. Surreptitiously Joe Harper kept an eye on his pocket watch.

At the same time Officer Burland stood tensely in Rockefeller Center's largest conference room. The twenty foot tall room boasted a vaulted ceiling that reminded the young cop of some sort of church sanctuary. In the rest of the venue Art Deco seemed to be in mortal conflict with the newer Art Nouveau style.

Dressed in waiter's livery, he had received only a quick lesson on taking care of the coffee and pastry layout for the meeting of the Civil Defense Committee. Burland had met one or two Committee members. He hoped nobody recognized him. At ten minutes before eleven o'clock he saw Gerald Orbach slide unobtrusively into the room. The unusual looking man placed his wide brimmed fedora on a side table and approached.

"Ready, Burland?" he said softly.

"As I'll ever be, sir. The special stuff is installed. The rest is under the skirt of the table we're standing by. The only problem I see is that the Mayor isn't here, yet."

"Then I may have to vamp a bit, until he arrives. When the surprise comes, you'll know what to do."

"I hope so, sir"

"You won't have any doubts. I'm sure of that. Ah, here's His Honor now."

New York Mayor Fiorello LaGuardia breezed into the room with only his NYPD detective bodyguard. He tossed his Homburg hat on the table next to the Green Ghost's fedora. Soon Burland heard the Mayor's strangely squeaky voice greeting various people. Not long after Commissioner Standish approached His Honor. The top cop bent down, for he towered over the five-foot-two-inch politician. A moment later LaGuardia called for everyone to be seated.

The Committee members found their places at the U-shaped arrangement of tables. "I'm told we have a special event on our program today," began the Mayor. "Commissioner Standish, please get us started."

Standish rose. "We meet every two weeks to help in keeping our city and its people safe. Some call the idea of Civil Defense alarmist or provocative. Well, let me tell you, there are reasons to be alarmed. I now introduce a man who seeks both justice, and to protect our city, state and nation. You do not need to know his name, but, if you trust me, trust him." With that he pointed to the corner of the room where the Green Ghost stood.

"Gentlemen, good day. How many of you knew there was a murder here at the Center last weekend?... Good, good. Glad to see you are a well informed group. Did any of you wonder if that murdered man had anything to do with Civil Defense?

"Joseph Parkinson, the victim, was a respected civil servant. He also held an Amateur Radio Operator's License. In addition, he had what turned out to be an unhealthy amount of curiosity. Should a major war break out in Europe, Mr. Parkinson knew, like during the Great War, all amateur radio would be shuttered for the duration. Then he discovered someone apparently circumventing that potential rule. He died before he could report his discovery."

Not too far away from the conference room Tiny Tim Terry fingered one of the three small automatic pistols he carried. He listened to his friend's discourse over headphones. *Just about time,* he thought. He raised the cover over a bank of four switches.

Over on Vinegar Hill the party behind the Robbins mansion gathered steam. Singing broke out. Then, at precisely five minutes to eleven, a work party pulled up almost in front of the mansion. Six men climbed out. A compressor roared as they attacked the surface of the street with a jackhammer. One block up the hill ten men waited silently behind the curtains of Mrs. Hutchinson's front parlor. The proper time approached. At CPO Fournier's whispered order they carefully put their hostess's coffee cups in a safe place, then picked up their gear. At two minutes to eleven three men hidden in the bushes on the mansion's west side began pelting the boarded up windows with ball bearings using heavy slingshots. At exactly eleven o'clock Joe Harper, and his companions, put down their bottles, grabbed wrecking bars and rushed to the back of the mansion.

Back at Rockefeller Center the Green Ghost paused to let the implications of his words set in. He surreptitiously gave a prearranged signal to Officer Burland. The young cop moved to the center of the conference room's north wall.

"Gentlemen," the Green Ghost continued, "in spite of what the well meaning Isolationists say, a secret war is already in progress against the Untied States of America. I will now introduce you to some of our enemies. *Fire for effect!*"

Within the guts of the building Tim Terry threw the four switches as quickly as he could.

Up in the vaulted ceiling area of the conference room came sharp cracks and popping noises. The startled sounds made of the Civil Defense Committee disappeared as plaster and lathing snapped and showered the four corners of the room. Then came the harsh yells of terrified men.

Looking at the rear of the room, Mayor LaGuardia watched open mouthed as a man fell through both corners of the fancy curving ceiling. With them fell pads of yellow paper, many pencils and a few wires. One man hit the carpet of the room like a belly-flop dive. The second managed to get his feet under him, but rolled forward when he landed.

Glancing to either side LaGuardia gasped. On his left another man held on to part of a shattered two-by-four for dear life. His feet dangled a dozen feet above the floor. To his right yet another man kept a strong grip on a brace as he fumbled for a gun holstered in the small of his back. The Mayor saw Inspector Cramer, his bodyguard, throw off his shock to yank out his Smith and Wesson Detective Special.

"Touch that gun," bellowed Cramer, "and you're dead!" The man stopped moving.

At that point the splintered two-by-four gave out. The third man managed to land crouched on his feet. Before he could stand he stared almost cross-eyed at the muzzle of Officer Burland's snub-nosed revolver. With his left hand Burland pitched a set of handcuffs to land at Inspector Cramer's feet. Pulling another set out of his pocket Burland began to secure his prisoner.

"Touch that gun and you're dead!"

Assessing the overall scene the Green Ghost raced toward the second man as he came out of his summersault. The man reached for something. The Green Ghost smashed a flash ball three feet in front of the man. Stunned, the spy froze amid the smoke. An instant later a flying forearm slammed his head into the wall. Barely a second after that a pair of handcuffs landed next to him. Another set followed almost immediately. *The kid's got a good arm,* thought the Green Ghost with a grim smile.

With all four men in manacles the Green Ghost headed for the speaker's podium by the main door. A quick glance showed him that Officer Burland had installed the special device properly. He pulled the cord to activate the thing, then counted to three.

"Gentlemen!" the Green Ghost called sharply from the podium. All heads turned in his direction. At that moment bright sparkly things and a huge ball of smoke enveloped the area.

George Chance dashed from the room. He threw open the door of a nearby broom closet. "You're on!" he whispered as he hurried towards the elevators.

Glenn Saunders, looking exactly like the Green Ghost, stood at the podium as the smoke finished clearing. Glancing around he saw three handcuffed men being herded towards him. A fourth man moved in the same direction, dragged by his feet.

Glenn often impersonated George Chance. Never had audiences, reporters or even casual acquaintances penetrated the deception. This seemed different. These men were fully alert. A large number of them were trained observers. Not to mention cops or military men. He knew the Green Ghost now dashed after the leader of this operation. His friend wanted to bring down the man personally. George Chance's hard scrabble circus upbringing prepared him for fighting and danger. Glenn's not so much. He nodded slightly at Admiral Woodward, then he began to speak.

Out on Vinegar Hill Joe Harper's team quietly slipped the tips of ice cold crowbars into a section of wall enclosing the former portico at the rear of the Robbins mansion. When the second hand of his pocket watch hit thirty seconds after eleven Joe dropped his hand. His companions' muscles bulged as they strained against the crowbars.

CPO Fournier and three others rushed between the houses separating the Hutchinson home from the mansion. As they crossed the street each man drew a Colt Model 1911 automatic. Two stood on each side for the front door. They watched as their six companions reached the street. The six paused only long enough to get a firmer grip on what they carried. Then they charged the door. The canvas wrapped railroad cross-tie barely slowed as the door smashed open. The six men dived to the side. The tie flew completely into the mansion. The Chief and his companions entered with weapons at the ready. The other six drew their own automatics and followed. They spread out to search the house.

The Green Ghost reached the elevators. The doors to one car shaft sported a neat "Out of Service" placard. Quickly he applied a special key to a tiny opening in the door. A hard shove revealed an elevator car ready to go. Closing the outer and inner doors he spun the control handle to full power going up. As he watched the floor numbers change he realized Glenn Saunders would now be addressing the Committee.

"These men," proclaimed Glenn Saunders, "and others like them, have been listening to every meeting held in this and the Center's other meeting rooms. They are stenographers. You looked for hidden microphones. The most these spies needed was a stethoscope when people talked in a low voice.

"Nor is listening here the group's only project. Even as I speak others are investigating possible sabotage near the Brooklyn Navy Yard…"

The screech of protesting heavy nails heralded the breaching of the back portico wall at the Robbins mansion. Two Marines grabbed one edge of the wall section and pulled sharply. Ducking through the slanted opening Joe Harper and Randy Heath scrambled inside with weapons drawn. Flattening themselves on the cobblestone floor they looked around.

To their left stood the original wall of the mansion. Nothing moved in that direction. The ten man team would be checking out the house. To the right most of the walls of the former stables had been demolished. Huge piles of dirt and large balks of wood filled the open area. Straight ahead lay an almost twenty foot diameter hole in the cobblestones. A set of wooden stairs hugged the far wall going down. Heavy wood timbers spanned the hole ten feet above the floor. Three different block and tackle rigs hung from the timbers. But nothing moved. A small amount of noise reverberated from the hole.

Joe looked at Heath. "Everybody in the pit?" he whispered.

The Green Ghost came through the door of the *Who's In Town* offices with his gun in one hand behind his back and his police credentials in the other. He managed to hold the ID wallet and put his index finger to his lips before Gloria, the receptionist, could greet him. Her eyes widened as he stepped toward her desk.

"Grab your purse," whispered the strange looking man in the dark green suit. "Go see the guard in the building lobby. Stay down there, please. Things could get rough up here. Go!"

Gloria looked from the man's intense face to the wallet he held for her to see. She nodded, snatched her purse from under her desk and headed out the door. The Green Ghost locked the outer door.

"Herbert Johnston!" called out the Green Ghost. "The time has come for Justice."

The Green Ghost stood his ground. For all of five carefully counted seconds. Then he kicked in the executive's door. He found Herbert Johnson tapping frantically on the back wall of the big closet.

Frank Miller, real name Mueller, crawled and climbed desperately through the guts of Rockefeller Center. His mind roiled as his luck, both good and bad. If his stenographic skills had been tested last week, as originally planned, he would have been one of the four men now in custody. As it was he had lain in the duct behind Roland, the team's leader, listening through a long stethoscope while scribbling shorthand.

As a new prisoner in the Great War, he had been processed next to an Allied artillery unit. He knew that "Fire for Effect!" meant explosions. Instinctively he curled up in a ball. Then came sharp sounds and Roland's bellow of fear and anger. Wood splinters tore at the backs of his hands as they covered his head. He looked up to see Roland gone and the conference room visible. He barely managed to turn his body around. He prayed he did not become lost in the still unfamiliar maze of ductwork. Good luck stood with him in that he did not pass Tiny Tim's hiding place. Tim would have shot him.

In the dim light of the closet Herbert Johnson barely took note of the intruder's gun. The man's death's head face terrified him. The man's lips reappeared as the Green Ghost spoke. Johnson did not notice.

"Herbert Johnson, you have no German ancestry. You are a registered Republican. Why have you betrayed your country?"

As the other Marines eased their way into the portico area Joe Harper looked around. When inclosing the portico, walls had simply been dropped from existing eves of the structure. Windows from three levels of the mansion still looked out onto the area. Suddenly one window at the third level slid up a few inches.

"Damn it!" hissed Joe as he brought up his .38 automatic.

As he spoke the muzzle of some sort of long gun appeared in the opening. All of his companions carried pistols. Now the bore of the weapon's barrel seemed big around as a beer bottle pointed straight at his head. Cursing a blue streak, Joe triggered his automatic four times.

Joe Harper's first round shattered the third floor window. The second gouged the windowsill. The third and fourth slugs entered the wall just below the rifle barrel. Suddenly the long gun pointed at the portico ceiling. At the same time Heath hand signaled two of the Marines to search the stable area while the rest covered the cistern.

Joe scanned all the windows of the mansion that overlooked the enclosed portico. Suddenly light flared in the room with the shattered window. The sound of three muffled shots reached him.

A few seconds later a voice bellowed through the window, "Hold Fire, Leathernecks!" Then the rifle's barrel disappeared. Unseen hands raised the remains of the shattered sash.

Commander Dawson appeared at the window. "First three floors clear," he called. "Still checking the basement."

Just then a voice came up from the cistern, "Salinger, what the Hell's going on?"

Joe and Heath looked up at Commander Dawson. The Coast Guardsman drew his flat hand sharply across his throat.

Heath nodded grimly. "Salinger's dead," he called out sharply.

"Dead?" came the faint reply. The speaker paused briefly. "Who's up there?"

Joe Harper almost broke out laughing as Heath thundered, "The Navy, the Marines and the Coast Guard!"

"Holy Hell! We surrender."

At the edge of the cistern on Vinegar Hill Chief Fournier joined Joe and Heath as the digging crew climbed the stairs with their hands up.

"Looks like two men watched the operation and cooked for these guys. Both pulled guns. With them dead the Commander's going over the plans we found to figure things out. Glad this operation is about over I'll take sea duty over this, any time."

Heath smiled and stretched while keeping an eye on the diggers as they were handcuffed. "Even though this is my home neighborhood, I agree with you Chief."

At Rockefeller Center Herbert Johnson looked straight into the Green Ghost's unblinking eyes. "I didn't know I'd betrayed my country. Not at first. When the new owners hired me to produce the show they said they wanted nothing to go on the air favoring international entanglements. I agreed with that idea. I lost a brother and two cousins in the trenches. I have two sons almost at draft age. I don't want them in danger.

"Everything seemed fine for the first few weeks. Then the studio rebuild happened and the spying started. They told me they'd make sure I took the blame for the whole thing. Like I dreamed it up in the first place."

"Then Joseph Parkinson started asking questions," said the Green Ghost. He did not hear the door to guts of the building open behind him.

"Yes," replied Johnson. "He discovered their sub-carrier test broadcasts. He couldn't understand what went out. Figured it might just be Lamont network business. I was trying to play along with that idea. It just happened that Roland, the leader of the listeners, stepped into my office to smoke a Lucky in the reception area. Next thing I knew he'd knifed Parkinson, then opened the secret door and shoved him in. He told me if he'd kill me if I talked, then he'd kill my family."

As the Green Ghost framed his next question Frank Mueller landed on his back.

At that same moment Tiny Tim Terry slipped out out of a secret exit into a third floor broom closet. Yesterday he and Merry White had modified the exit so that a normal sized man could not use it. They had also securely bolted two of the other three exits shut. Tim upended an empty mop pail. He sat on the bottom, two automatics in his lap, just in case someone tried to break out.

One arm circled the Green Ghost's neck. With his other hand the man slammed the point of a sharp pencil into the Green Ghost's right wrist. His gun went flying under Johnson's desk.

The Green Ghost bent his knees, then sprang up. As soon as his feet cleared the floor he nearly dived into a forward roll. The two bodies rotated a full two-hundred-seventy degrees. Mueller landed on his back just as the Green Ghost came down on top of him, smashing his left elbow into the attacker's rib-cage.

A bit groggy, himself, the Green Ghost rolled in the direction of the desk. Gun now in hand, he looked around to take stock. Mueller struggled to breathe. Of Herbert Johnson there was no sign. Yanking some thin but strong magician's silk scarves from a pocket, he quickly tied Mueller up. Seeing the door to the hall still locked, he knew where to find his quarry.

Herbert Johnson risked life and limb as he scrambled through Rockefeller Center's air ducts. Unlike the very cautious listeners, he didn't care if anybody heard him. He descended five floors and crossed to a telephone closet on the opposite side of the huge building. He slowed down to quietly approach the false wall section. The mechanism worked perfectly. He slid down into the wire closet feet first on his belly. In the darkness he turned around and gasped.

Illuminated in a dim green glow Death's own face waited for him.

"Herbert Johnson, you will not escape justice that easily!"

In the Rectory George Chance and his friends dined on Middle Eastern fare from Nabil's Ceders of Lebanon restaurant in the area below Canal Street.

Finishing a bite of felafel Merry White asked, "Did you actually solve the murder, lover?"

"Yes," replied George. "Johnson, the producer, will testify against the whole operation. That includes the killer, if his family is protected."

"What exactly were the Nazis doing at the mansion?" Tim Terry asked as he speared a small stuffed vine-leaf with his fork.

"Turned out," said Joe Harper, "they weren't Nazis, or Bundists, the people digging, that is. They're an out of work sandhog crew. Didn't know exactly where they were. Thought they might be tunneling into a bank or jewelers vault. They were living in the mansion with a pair of Bundists keeping an eye on them. Those two tried to shoot it out. They died.

"Just before I left Heath told me the dig's objective was to get under the main magazines at the Navy Yard. A small charge placed there could set off all the Navy's stored munitions. Would'a blown most of the Yard higher that up! Including the new battleship that's almost done. Remember, during the Great War, the big blast up in Halifax, Nova Scotia? That one was heard all the way to Boston. This would have been bigger, and in a much more populated area. Commander Dawson figured a week to ten days, tops, and ka-blam."

George Chance picked up his glass of wine. "We've done very well, my friends. But I fear there will be many more threats to this nation of ours. Now, a toast to Joseph Parkinson, a patriotic man who died for his country."

The sound of clinking glasses filled the Rectory parlor.

THE END

FINALLY, THE GREEN GHOST...
WITH THANKS TO ED KESSELL

first met the Green Ghost with the help of long time fan, and organizer of the first PulpCon, Ed Kessell. I got to know Ed through the old Ozark Science Fiction Association just before the St. Louis Worldcon in 1969 where he ran the dealer room.

At that time I was finishing college. My experience with the hero-pulps consisted mostly of Doc Savage, Phantom Detective, and Secret Agent X paperback reprints plus a small stack of Shadow pulps along with a couple of Spiders, a single Captain Future and Masked Rider. Ed knew I wanted to try others.

I snuck into the Worldcon Dealer Room a few minutes early on opening day. As Ed cheerfully threw me back out he pointed to a table near the door and told me the fellow had an early issue of the Green Ghost at a bargain price. So I bought it. I believe it was issue #3. The title: *Murder Makes a Ghost*. In it I met George Chance and company for the first time.

More than once I've heard fans say that most of the pulp heroes published by the Thrilling / Standard / Pines group of magazines were fairly interchangeable. That is a base story could be written, then, with the same amount of effort, that tale could star the Phantom Detective, the Crimson Mask, or the Masked Detective.

The same can not be said of the Green Ghost. G.T. Fleming-Roberts worked hard to make a different type of hero. And, after the first few stories, he got to use his own well established by-line, instead of a house name.

Here's how it got started. Master stage magician George Chance met Commissioner Standish and they hit it off. George then went for what today is known as a police ride-along on a puzzling case. He solved that case and Standish said he might call on him again. Now, in George Chances own words: "In the days and weeks that followed, I found one concept more and more dominating my thoughts -- Magic and Crime-Detection. How to merge the two and make them one. And so, not all at once, but gradually, slowly--but surely--the idea of the Green Ghost took form."

I should note that a large majority of the Green Ghost's cases were narrated in the third person. Airship 27 elected to have our new tales told that way. However, in 1940, the first few adventures were told in the first person. The quote above is from George Chance's first recorded case *Calling the Ghost* from January 1940.

There is lots of room to tell new stories about George Chance and his friends. George's crime hunting alter-ego is well established by the beginning of 1940. Maybe I'll find another case that will interest the Green Ghost. I hope so.

ERWIN K. ROBERTS - has now been retired for about a year. A Missouri resident nearly all his life, he doesn't mind traveling. He still has four, or is it five, states he has not spent any time in. Not to mention he wants to see his wife's former country, Lebanon. And lots of other places. Erwin has been, in no particular order, a cable TV personality, an air-defense missile radar operator, an urban redevelopment business re-locator, a switchboard operator and a Boy Scout camp councilor. He's also worked in a ceramics studio, a truck aftermarket shop, and a couple of graphic arts and sign studios.

He and his wife of over forty years have two adult kids who seem in no hurry to make them grandparents. Lots of money would be nice, but Erwin mostly writes for the love of creating. In fact, he needs to have something creative on his plate all the time. In addition to writing his own characters, he relishes the chance to write new adventures of characters he enjoyed back in the day. The Green Ghost now joins the company of the Masked Rider, the Phantom Detective, Sinbad and a couple of others. Not every one of them is published yet. The important part is crafting the stories.

FROM MAGIC TO CRIME SOLVING

Magicians turned crime fighters have always been the stuff of grand pulp adventures going all the way back to Lee Falk's classic strip hero, Mandrake the Magician. Even the real life magician/escape artist Harry Houdini appeared in dime novels featuring his fictional exploits and went on to star in a silent screen serial. There's just something about a practitioner of prestidigitation fighting villainy that appeals to our imagination.

Of all such fictional magicians turned vigilante, none was more colorful and dramatic than George Chance, aka the Green Ghost as created by writer G.T. Fleming-Roberts. Initially he was merely the Ghost: Super Detective; a title used by several popular pulp characters. Eventually to set him apart, he was referred to as the Green Ghost which played to his greenish skull make-up that he would don to frighten his enemies. It was just plain creepy.

Chance had been raised in the circus: his father was an animal trainer and his mother a trapeze artist. During his early life under the Big-Top, he mastered such skills as knife throwing, ventriloquism and, finally, stage magic. It was the latter he excelled in and upon reaching manhood left the traveling circus for the lights of Vaudeville where he started his own review and was soon acclaimed as one of the greatest magicians in the land.

Along the way Chance assembled an eclectic group of followers who would become his closest friends and allies. The lovely socialite brunette Merry White was his lady: a former glamour girl with both keen intelligence and fearless courage despite her small stature. It was her green eyes that mesmerized the magician.

Then there was Tiny Tim Terry, a midget also a veteran circus star and Chance's oldest friend and confidant. He often served as Chance's chief investigator. There was the irascible Joe Harper, a one time bookmaker, booking agent and gambler. It was said he knew Broadway inside out. Glenn Saunders was Chance's identical double and upon meeting the young, would-be magician, Chance realized Saunders would prove invaluable by doubling for the magician, allowing him to become the Green Ghost. Thus no one would ever be able to connect the bizarre vigilante with George Chance, retired stage magician.

There were two others who became privy to Chance's secret identity and both helped him in many of the Green Ghost mysteries: Police Commissioner Edward Standish and Chief Medical Examiner, Dr. Robert Demarest.

Chance's disguise was easily one of the most dramatic in all of pulp history. George Chance was an impressive, handsome man at six-feet one with broad shoulders, a trim waist, blue eyes, gold-colored hair, a broad forehead, thin mouth and nose with prominent cheekbones. To transform himself into the Green Ghost, he went underwent a rigorous make-up procedure. Small oval wires were inserted into his nose, tilting the lips and elongating the nostrils. Brown eye-shadow was used to darken his eye-pits. A powder gave the effect of a sickly pallor to his skin. He highlighted his cheek bones and over his teeth he placed celluloid the color of old yellowed ivory. He had only to part his lips in a skull-like grin, affect a fixed stare with deeply sunken eyes looking blank and his face, under a small green light hidden his collar, became ghastly, like that of an animated green skull. Of course he continued to wear a special suit containing secret pockets for his magic tricks in addition to an automatic, though he was a bad shot and preferred to use the throwing knife hidden in his right sleeve.

Using all the skills he had mastered both on stage and in the circus, George Chance was a formidable combatant in the war against crime and his exploits as the eerie Green Ghost were easily some of the most fondly remembered pulp tales of all time. Now Airship 27 Productions takes great joy in bringing Chance & Co. back to action in four brand new thrilling tales by today's hottest new pulp scribes: Michael Panush, Greg Hatcher, B.C. Bell and Erwin K. Roberts. Add moody, atmospheric illustrations by artist Zachary Brunner and we think we've got a package that would have made G.T. Fleming-Roberts proud. We hope you'll agree and let us know if you would like us to continue this series.

Thanks as ever for your continued support.

Ron Fortier
2/28/2014
Fort Collins, CO
(www.airship27.com)
(Airship27@comcast.net)

www.ingramcontent.com/pod-product-compliance
Lightning Source LLC
Chambersburg PA
CBHW071240250626
47163CB00001B/268